Moon Craft Down!

"What do we do now?" Miss Pickerell asked in an awe-struck voice.

"We wait," Foster said. "The base is bound to track us down. They'll send a rescue ship."

Miss Pickerell tried to push the thought out of her head, but she could not help remembering about the oxygen packs. Forty minutes was the limit that she, Foster, and her cat, Pumpkins, could remain on the moon's surface and survive. . . .

"The rescue ship is probably on its way already," Foster said reassuringly.

Miss Pickerell looked down at the ground. She didn't want Foster to see the trouble in her eyes. He seemed to have forgotten that their radar system was no longer working. How could the rescue ship even know where to begin to look for them?

#1

Miss Pickerell on the Moon

by Ellen MacGregor and Dora Pantell
Illustrated by Charles Geer

AN ARCHWAY PAPERBACK
POCKET BOOKS • NEW YORK

POCKET BOOKS, a Simon & Schuster division of
GULF & WESTERN CORPORATION
1230 Avenue of the Americas, New York, N.Y. 10020

Copyright © 1965 by McGraw-Hill, Inc.

Published by arrangement with McGraw-Hill Book Company
Library of Congress Catalog Card Number: 64-66411

ISBN: 0-671-56068-9

First Pocket Books printing January, 1980

10 9 8 7 6 5 4 3 2 1

Trademarks registered in the United States and other countries.

Printed in the U.S.A.

To Jack Goldfarb,
earth traveler, whose participation helped
to make this space journey possible.

Contents

Miss Pickerell
on the Moon

The motorcycle was coming closer.

1
Miss Pickerell Meets a Space Detective

Miss Pickerell was busy putting a last coat of pink paint on the outside of her farmhouse on Square Toe Mountain when she heard the sound of a motorcycle. She hoped it wasn't coming her way. She had too much to think about at this moment to entertain any visitors. Tomorrow was her cow's birthday. She planned to have her house all clean and shining by then. Miss Pickerell looked across the peaceful valley to the pasture where her cow was quietly grazing in the sunshine and sighed with contentment. It was a beautiful morning. If tomorrow turned out to be anywhere near as nice, her cow would have a perfect birthday.

The motorcycle was coming closer. Miss Pickerell could hear the whirr distinctly. And as it approached the turn in her private road, she could see the green and orange colors that identified it as belonging to Mr. Humwhistel, Square Toe City's new schoolteacher. Miss Pickerell remembered that her seven nieces and nephews adored Mr. Humwhistel.

"But I don't understand why he should be coming to see me," she said, as she vigorously tucked a loose hairpin into place.

Miss Pickerell could see him clearly now, his tie flying in the wind, his old-fashioned vest buttoned tightly up to his neck, his gold-rimmed glasses looking as though they were about to fall off his nose at any minute. She could also see that Mr. Esticott who had just been promoted from train conductor to baggage master was sitting in the sidecar. Mr. Esticott was hugging a shoe box against his chest. What's more, for some strange reason he was leaning over the box and talking to it.

The motorcycle roared up the road and came to a sputtering stop outside the farmyard gate. Mr. Esticott was the first to get off.

2

Miss Pickerell reluctantly put down the paintbrush, took off her gloves, and went to open the gate.

"Good morning, Miss Pickerell," Mr. Esticott said. "The mail train just brought this package. I'm so glad it came in time. And I'm grateful to Mr. Humwhistel for giving me a lift. Today is your cow's birthday, isn't it? Congratulations!"

"Tomorrow," Miss Pickerell said, as she nodded an answer to Mr. Humwhistel's greeting. "My cow will be twelve years old tomorrow."

"Time does fly," Mr. Esticott remarked, still holding on to the box.

Miss Pickerell was wondering what could be in it. She did not like to ask.

Mr. Esticott cleared his throat.

"Miss Pickerell," he continued. "I've been trying for months to think of some way to thank you for letting me read and reread your encyclopedia. I realize it took me a long time, especially the P volume, because I was so very much interested in the information it had about the planets. You may have been right, though, when you suggested once that I was a slow reader."

3

"I'm sure of it," Miss Pickerell said. "You kept that volume for five weeks. And I kept telling you how much I needed it."

"Yes," said Mr. Esticott, sighing. "And to show my appreciation, I've brought your cow a birthday present. Or rather, I had my daughter in Plentibush City buy it and send it to me. It's a kitten. A male kitten."

He lifted the cover off the box.

Miss Pickerell looked down into the big

yellow eyes of a very black kitten with two round white spots on his forehead. The kitten looked back at her timidly.

"Mercy!" Miss Pickerell breathed. "Why, he's too frightened even to cry. I'd better give him some milk."

She picked the kitten up quickly and hurried across her freshly planted cucumber patch and up the wooden steps that led to the kitchen. She had him settled on a sunny window sill and halfway through his saucer of milk by the time the two men caught up.

"A kitten was a splendid idea," she exclaimed, as Mr. Esticott and Mr. Humwhistel entered the kitchen. "People so often have trouble thinking of a gift for a cow. I'm very grateful to you, Mr. Esticott."

"An animal should have a name!" Mr. Humwhistel said suddenly in a loud, clear voice. "Having a name means that someone has him and loves him."

Mr. Humwhistel stopped talking just as suddenly as he'd begun. He sat down in Miss Pickerell's kitchen rocker. Miss Pickerell thought he looked very pale.

"Aren't you feeling well?" she asked.

"Not too bad," he replied. "Coming up

into the altitude of these mountains some-times makes me a little dizzy. Change of air pressure can do that, you know.''

"I read in the A volume of the encyclo-pedia," Mr. Esticott said. "that the earth is surrounded by a blanket of air.''

Mr. Humwhistel laughed.

"Maybe it's not a very good blanket," he said. "It gets thinner the higher up you go. But then you know a lot about air pres-sure, don't you, Miss Pickerell? I under-stand you've been to Mars.''

"Will you have some peppermintade?" Miss Pickerell asked. She did not want to talk about Mars just now. She was too con-cerned about the way Mr. Humwhistel looked. She was also eager to get on with her painting and to go down to the pasture to visit her cow.

"I love peppermint," Mr. Humwhistel answered, smiling and looking better al-ready. "Now about that kitten. You could call him Pumpkins, short for 'My very ed-ucated mother just served us nine pump-kins.' ''

"My very educated mother just served us nine pumpkins?" Miss Pickerell re-peated. "My very educated mother—'' she

6

began again, hardly believing that she had heard it correctly.

"It's a nonsense sentence," Mr. Humwhistel explained. "I teach it to the children to help them remember the names of the planets. There are nine of them you know—Mercury, Venus, Earth, Mars, Jupiter, Saturn, Uranus, Neptune, and Pluto. Every work in the nonsense sentence begins with the first letter of a planet, '*M*y *V*ery *E*ducated *M*other *J*ust *S*erved *U*s *N*ine *P*umpkins.' "

"That's a wonderful idea," Miss Pickerell exclaimed admiringly.

"I like nonsense sentences," Mr. Humwhistel said. "I'm always making them up. And I think Pumpkins is a good name for a cat."

"Hmm—Pumpkins, Pumpkins," Miss Pickerell said, trying the name out on her tongue. It sounded just right, somehow.

"You're probably a very good teacher," she said to Mr. Humwhistel. "Tell me—"

She had no chance to finish. A low and very distinct mooing sound was coming from the direction of the pasture. Miss Pickerell looked anxiously up at the electric clock on the wall.

"It's my cow," she said. "This is the time of day when I usually go out and talk to her."

"I'll go," Mr. Esticott offered. "I'll take Pumpkins with me so that they can get acquainted."

"Please," Miss Pickerell said, hoping that her cow wouldn't think she had forgotten her. "And tell her I'll be there very soon."

She turned to Mr. Humwhistel. He was busy getting his pipe out of the pocket of his jacket. He had turned the pocket inside out. Miss Pickerell noticed that there were three holes in it.

She was becoming very impatient. It really was growing late and Mr. Humwhistel gave no signs of getting ready to leave. He just rocked back and forth.

"Are you enjoying your work at the school?" Miss Pickerell asked, when she felt she had to say something.

"Very much," Mr. Humwhistel answered. "It's hard to do two jobs at once, though."

"What other job do you do?" Miss Pickerell asked. Mr. Humwhistel had a most mysterious way of explaining things.

"Why, I work for the Space Exploration people. I'm a—a—" Hr. Humwhistel seemed to be hunting for the right word. "I suppose you might call me a space detective," he said, finally, smiling a little.

"A space detective!" Miss Pickerell gasped. "What—what do you detect?"

"Messages that our space stations radio back to earth," Mr. Humwhistel told her. "I also help decode the messages and relay them to other scientists for study. The program began about the time of your trip to Mars. We have a very reliable system for receiving messages from outer space by now."

"I see," said Miss Pickerell, who wasn't entirely sure that she did. "What kind of messages are they?"

"Various kinds," Mr. Humwhistel said. "Some are about the weather. I think you will be happy to know that we will soon be able to predict the weather for months in advance. That's because our television-equipped satellites from out in space send us information about temperature and clouds and storms."

Miss Pickerell hoped this was so. She liked to plan ahead, and unexpected weather changes could be very upsetting.

"Some of our stations have been sending us far more important information," Mr. Humwhistel went on. "One of the messages I decoded last week was from our new micro-biological laboratory on the moon. It was about the possible discovery of molds on the moon's surface. Molds are tiny plants that—"

"Excuse me," Miss Pickerell interrupted. "I know all about molds. My middle nephew, Euphus, has been growing them on pieces of bread for years. But I think you must be mistaken about molds on the moon. Molds can't grow on the moon. Nothing grows on the moon."

"You are quite right," Mr. Humwhistel said, nodding emphatically. "But these are not growing molds. They're mold spores, which are like seeds. We're not really sure where they came from. Maybe from outer space. Anyway, our scientists in the moon laboratory feel very hopeful about them. They think the spores can grow into molds which produce antibiotics. And the antibiotics may cure some germ diseases we don't know too much about treating."

Miss Pickerell remembered that penicillin came from a mold and how quickly it had helped her when she was so sick with a nasty infection two winters ago. Who could tell what these new moon molds might do! She understood why her nieces and nephews were so fond of Mr. Humwhistel. A teacher and a space detective, too!

"I wish I knew more about all the exciting things scientists are doing today," Miss Pickerell said.

"Would you be interested in seeing some of the messages we've been getting from our satellites and spacecraft?" Mr. Humwhistel asked. "I have a few with me. They're old ones that I've been showing to the class."

"Thank you," Miss Pickerell said. "I'd love to see them."

Mr. Humwhistel took some wrinkled scraps of paper from a jacket pocket. He spread them carefully on the white kitchen table.

Miss Pickerell opened her eyes wide and stared. There were no words on the paper, only lines that went up and down like funny little waves.

"This message," Mr. Humwhistel began, pointing to one especially crumpled scrap, "came from the spacecraft that we sent up in Operation Moon Shot to explore conditions. We needed to know more about the surface of the moon before we built the first manned moon-bound spaceship. That's when we learned that a landing could be managed where the dust was not too thick on the rocks. And now, let's have a look at these wavy little lines, shall we?"

Mr. Humwhistel was just beginning to explain to Miss Pickerell what the lines meant when a sudden shout made them both rush to the window. It was Mr. Esticott.

"Miss Pickerell! Miss Pickerell!" he was calling at the top of his lungs. "Miss Pickerell, there's something wrong with your cow. Her legs can barely hold her up! Her tongue is hanging out! And she's trying to moo, trying with all her might, but she can hardly make a sound."

2
What Is Wrong with the Cow?

Miss Pickerell found her cow standing quietly in the clover of the lower pasture when she, Mr. Esticott, and Mr. Humwhistel got down there.

"She—she looks all right to me," Miss Pickerell said, trying to catch her breath after running so fast.

Mr. Esticott looked embarrassed.

"I'm sorry," he said.

"Sorry!" Miss Pickerell exclaimed. "See here, Mr. Esticott—"

"I mean I'm sorry I upset you," Mr. Esticott explained. "She looked very sick just a few minutes ago."

"She doesn't seem to be eating," Mr.

13

Humwhistel observed. "I don't know much about cows. I always understood, though, that they ate all the time when they were put out to pasture."

"They eat when they're hungry," Miss Pickerell said, "which is more than I can say about some people I know. My oldest niece, Rosemary, can never say 'no' to candy."

Miss Pickerell patted her cow's head and stroked her neck. The cow mooed very, very softly.

"It would help if she could talk," Mr. Esticott said. "Then she'd be able to tell you what's the matter with her."

"Animals talk," Mr. Humwhistel said. "They talk with their eyes, with their ears, with their tails—with everything. Look at the way she's twitching her nose now, Miss Pickerell. Does she often do that?"

"No," Miss Pickerell said.

"And her eyes," Mr. Humwhistel went on. "She seems to be squinting."

"I do that myself, sometimes," Mr. Esticott suggested, "when the sun's in my eyes and I don't have my dark glasses on."

"The sun is not in her eyes, Mr. Esticott," Miss Pickerell said. "And I'm sure

14

that Dr. Haggerty, my veterinarian, would have prescribed dark glasses for her if he'd thought she needed them. My cow gets a thorough physical check-up at least once a year. Dr. Haggerty said she was in excellent condition the last time he examined her."

A loud meow came from the raspberry bushes that bordered Miss Pickerell's meadow.

The cow mooed weakly again. She put her head down and grumbled.

"It's Pumpkins," Mr. Esticott said. "The meowing disturbs her."

Pumpkins made his way out of the bushes and strolled over to the cow. He sniffed her daintily. The cow licked his coat.

"They're friends," Miss Pickerell said. "Something else is bothering her."

She patted the cow again. "Her head feels a little warm," she said.

"You might put a mustard plaster on her chest." Mr. Esticott suggested. "My mother used to do that when I had a cold."

"We don't know if she has a cold, Mr. Esticott," Miss Pickerell said. "Anyway, with all the new drugs we have today, we don't need to use anything as uncomfort-

able as a mustard plaster. We know much more about medicines than we used to.''

''We still don't know everything,'' Mr. Humwhistel sighed. ''I wish we did.''

Miss Pickerell went on looking at her cow.

The cow suddenly opened her mouth and bellowed.

Mr. Esticott jumped back in surprise.

Mr. Humwhistel blinked several times.

Miss Pickerell said, "She's sick. She's really sick. She's trying to tell us what's wrong. Excuse me. I must go and call Dr. Haggerty immediately."

"Perhaps you'd better stay with your cow, Miss Pickerell," Mr. Humwhistel said gently. "I'll telephone Dr. Haggerty for you, if you like."

"That's very kind of you," Miss Pickerell said. "His number is on the kitchen bulletin board."

Mr. Humwhistel ran quickly up to the house.

Miss Pickerell spoke soothingly to her cow. "It's all right," she told her. "Dr. Haggerty will be here soon. He'll make you feel better."

Mr. Esticott said "Hmmm." He cleared his throat two or three times. He coughed.

"Aren't you feeling well either?" Miss Pickerell asked, looking at him a little curiously.

"I'm feeling fine," Mr. Esticott said stiffly. "I'm just trying to make up my mind about whether I should say something to you."

"Well!" Miss Pickerell exclaimed.

Mr. Esticott coughed again.

"I hope you won't mind my bringing this up," he said finally. "But I think you should ask Covington, my substitute signalman, to come and take a look at your cow. Why, he found a half-starved stray dog and turned it into the liveliest animal in town. He taught him enough tricks to get a vaudeville booking at the Square Toe City Picture—''

Miss Pickerell did not let him finish.

"Just because Covington is your cousin," she said, indignantly, "is no reason for—"

Mr. Esticott did not let her finish either.

"He's not my cousin," he retorted. "You're thinking of Foster, the one who used to be a bush pilot. He's got a new job now. It's very special. He's on the moon, doing map studies. A selenodetic survey, I think they call it."

"Let's not change the subject," Miss Pickerell persisted. "Covington is an animal trainer, not an animal doctor. When my cow is sick, I want the best professional advice I can get for her."

"Dr. Haggerty has an excellent reputation," Mr. Esticott admitted. "Is he still with the circus?"

"No, he gave up being a circus veterinarian," Miss Pickerell said.

She stooped down to talk to her cow. "Dr. Haggerty understands you and loves you," she said reassuringly. "He'll know what to do."

19

Miss Pickerell looked at her watch.

"I wonder why it's taking Mr. Humwhistel so long to make the telephone call," she said.

Just then Mr. Humwhistel appeared over the top of the hill and came rushing toward them. He seemed very upset.

"What's the matter?" Miss Pickerell and Mr. Esticott asked, both at the same time.

"He can't come," Mr. Humwhistel said. "Dr. Haggerty can't come to see your cow."

"What!" Miss Pickerell exclaimed in a loud, unbelieving voice.

"He says he can examine her better in his office," Mr. Humwhistel explained. "He has the fluoroscope and the x-ray machine and all the other equipment that he needs right there."

"Oh!" Miss Pickerell said.

"But there's another reason he can't come," Mr. Humwhistel went on. "He can't spare the time. Half the animals in Square Toe City are down with some mysterious ailment. It looks like an epidemic, Miss Pickerell. We must get your cow ex-

amined immediately. We must get Pumpkins checked, too. Hurry, Miss Pickerell!
There's not a moment to lose!''

3
The Mysterious Epidemic

Mr. Humwhistel and Mr. Esticott accompanied Miss Pickerell on her trip to Dr. Haggerty's office. Miss Pickerell drove her car. Mr. Humwhistel sat next to her with Pumpkins on his lap. Mr. Esticott sat in the trailer with the cow. The trailer was red, with a little canvas awning for protection against bad weather.

Dr. Haggerty was waiting for them in the clean, tidy barn he used as an examining room. Miss Pickerell noticed that he looked tired and worried.

"Good afternoon, Dr. Haggerty," she said. "This is Mr. Humwhistel. He and Mr. Esticott were kind enough to come with me. And this is Pumpkins. He's a present from Mr. Esticott, who got him from his daughter. Perhaps you can check on Pumpkins if you have a chance."

"I'll examine your cow first," Dr. Haggerty said.

The examination was very quick. Dr. Haggerty took the cow's temperature, looked carefully into her throat, and listened to the sounds of her heart and lungs through the stethoscope that dangled from a long black ribbon around his neck. He gave Miss Pickerell the diagnosis while he was washing his hands with soap and disinfectant at the sink.

"I hate to tell you this, Miss Pickerell," he said, "but I'm afraid your cow has caught this infectious germ disease that's going the rounds."

"Oh," said Miss Pickerell, in a stifled, horrified voice.

Dr. Haggerty picked up a hypodermic syringe and began to sterilize it.

"Are you going to give my cow an injection?" Miss Pickerell asked.

"I'm going to give her an antibiotic," Dr. Haggerty replied. "An antibiotic mixed with a strong dose of vitamins. The vita-

mins are to give her some strength to fight
the disease. But—'' His voice trailed off
discouragingly.

Miss Pickerell stared at him.

''You mean—'' she said. ''You're trying
to tell me—'' She didn't finish her sentence
either.

Dr. Haggerty rubbed the cow's flank
with a dab of cotton and put the needle in.

Miss Pickerell patted her cow's head to
comfort her.

Dr. Haggerty looked up at Miss Pickerell. ''Let me explain something to you,''

he said. "The antibiotic I've just given your cow is an antigerm substance. That's what all antibiotics are. There are many different kinds of antibiotics. Some of them will destroy one germ, some another."

He paused. Miss Pickerell waited for him to go on.

"Miss Pickerell," he said, finally, "I must be frank with you. I've used one antibiotic after another in fighting this particular germ. Nothing seems to work. So far, the reaction of the animals to the medication I've been giving them has been very poor."

Miss Pickerell went white. "Isn't there anything you can do?" she pleaded.

"I can keep on trying," Dr. Haggerty sighed. He washed his hands and dried them on a clean towel.

"This is a highly infectious animal disease," he went on. "Let's hope your kitten hasn't caught it. I'll take a look at him now."

Mr. Humwhistel put Pumpkins down on the stainless-steel examining table. Pumpkins meowed his complaint.

"Has he been vaccinated yet?" Dr. Haggerty asked.

Miss Pickerell looked questioningly at Mr. Esticott.

"Vaccinated!" Mr. Esticott said in amazement. "Of course not! I'm sure I would have heard about it if my daughter had had him vaccinated."

"Vaccinations are most important," Miss Pickerell stated emphatically. "It's easy to see your daughter hasn't ever really had any animal friends."

"Vaccinations prevent certain virus diseases," Dr. Haggerty explained. "They serve to immunize the animal against these illnesses."

"Dr. Haggerty means that they keep the animal from getting that disease," Miss Pickerell said to Mr. Esticott.

Dr. Haggerty nodded. "The vaccine I inject helps the body manufacture chemicals which prevent the disease," he said. "An antibiotic, on the other hand, helps only to destroy a germ."

"I'm a strong believer in prevention myself," Mr. Esticott defended himself.

Pumpkins got both a vaccination and a vitamin shot.

"He seems healthy," Dr. Haggerty told Miss Pickerell. "I've given him vitamins

27

only as a general booster. When there is an epidemic like this one, all animals should get extra vitamins.''

"Yes," Miss Pickerell said.

"It's only fair to warn you, however," Dr. Haggerty added, "that this is a very widespread epidemic. Pumpkins may still come down with the disease. He may even have caught it and not be showing the symptoms as yet. I'll stop by on my way home tonight and take another look at him.''

Dr. Haggerty called for his nurse to come and lead the cow away. "Your cow will have to stay in isolation," he explained to Miss Pickerell.

"May I come and visit her?" Miss Pickerell asked, as she sadly stroked the cow's head.

"We'll see how she feels tomorrow," Dr. Haggerty said.

Miss Pickerell, Mr. Humwhistel, and Mr. Esticott said good-by to Dr. Haggerty and thanked him politely. Mr. Humwhistel, still holding Pumpkins, led the way back to the car. They passed a number of other animals and their owners who had arrived to see Dr. Haggerty. There were several tired-looking cats and dogs, a sad-eyed chimpanzee, a lame old plow horse, and two baby lambs huddling close to their mother.

Nobody spoke on the way home. Every once in a while Miss Pickerell looked back at the empty trailer rattling behind them and then blinked back the tears that stung her eyelids.

She drove slowly through the quiet countryside. The windows were open and she could smell the sweet honeysuckle and hear the buzzing chorus of bees in the fruit trees.

Suddenly, she jammed on the brakes. "I can't bear it," she said. "I can't bear not doing anything to help my cow. I must try and do *something*. For her and for the other animals."

"What?" Mr. Humwhistel and Mr. Esticott asked together.

Miss Pickerell thought for a moment. "I have an idea," she said.

"What?" Mr. Humwhistel asked this time.

"Well, it may not be the most startling idea in the world, Mr. Humwhistel," she admitted, "but—"

"What is it?" Mr. Esticott wanted to know.

"But it may help," she added decisively. "And it's certainly worth trying."

She smoothed her hair, sat up erect, and, looking considerably brighter, stepped firmly on the accelerator. For the first time in her life Miss Pickerell drove up Square Toe Mountain at a speed of more than twenty-five miles an hour.

4

A Most Amazing Plan

The moment Miss Pickerell got home she crossed the kitchen to the telephone on the wall. She was so excited, she didn't even stop to explain anything to Mr. Humwhistel and Mr. Esticott. They waited to say good-by to her. Mr. Humwhistel still held Pumpkins in his arms.

"I've never called my oldest niece Rosemary yet that the line hasn't been busy," Miss Pickerell said, as she hung up in exasperation. "I don't believe she ever gets off the phone."

She dialed the number again. This time, there was an answer.

"Rosemary," Miss Pickerell said. "I

have something terribly important to tell you. Can you hear me?''

Rosemary said that of course she could hear. Why was Miss Pickerell shouting?

"I'll tell you when you get here," Miss Pickerell said. "You can take the next bus. It leaves at 3:03. No, it's—"

With her free hand, she rapidly turned the pages of her timetable.

"It's 3:23," she continued. "That should get you here by 5:24. Please bring Homer and Harry with you. And leave a note for Dwight. Tell him I want to see him, too. Tell him to take the car. Tell him to bring his friends. I'll need all the help I can get. This is an emergency."

Miss Pickerell put the receiver back on the hook.

"I'll need your help, too," she said to Mr. Esticott and Mr. Humwhistel.

She walked quickly to the end of the large kitchen table where she kept her typewriter. For just an instant before she sat down, she looked out across the valley to the pasture and to the barn and the old apple orchard below. It seemed to her that she had never seen anything quite so lonely. Then she resolutely slid a piece of paper into the machine. She read aloud as she typed, CAMPAIGN FOR CONTROL OF EPIDEMIC.

"Ah!" Mr. Humwhistel said, sounding very interested. "Early diagnosis is most important."

Miss Pickerell acknowledged his suggestion with a nod of her head and typed, "All animals showing any abnormal symptoms whatever must be taken to veterinarian immediately. Early diagnosis essential."

"I could put up a poster about it in the baggage room," Mr. Esticott suggested.

Miss Pickerell typed, *"Dwight* to print posters to this effect and to distribute them for display in baggage room. Also in post office and supermarket. He can use my cardboard and borrow my India ink. If he prefers to use his Magic Marker, that's all right."

"If Mr. Humwhistel would lend me his motorcycle, I could notify some of the animal owners," Mr. Esticott went on. "I could go on my day off."

Mr. Humwhistel was walking around the room excitedly.

"We mustn't forget the well animals," he said. "As Dr. Haggerty recommended, they will need vitamin shots. And there's the problem of separating the healthy animals from the sick ones. If they live in the same place, something must be—"

Miss Pickerell signaled for him to wait a moment while she typed. "All well animals to be taken to veterinarian for vitamin injections. Animal owners to be notified. I suggest *Rosemary* for this. She can ask her Girl Scout troop to help her. *Mr. Esticott* will also help on his day off. Isolation for sick animals is most—"

She stopped. She couldn't think very well with the sound of Mr. Humwhistel's footsteps behind her. She turned around to ask him if he would sit down.

Mr. Humwhistel was just putting Pumpkins down on the horsehair sofa that stood in the hall. The kitten promptly curled himself up into a ball and went to sleep.

Miss Pickerell looked up at Mr. Humwhistel. He had somehow managed to lose two buttons off his coat on the way to and from Dr. Haggerty's office. His glasses were farther down on his nose than ever. He was fumbling in his pocket for his pipe. It all seemed to remind her of something. She couldn't quite put her finger on it.

Then, suddenly, she remembered what it was. A new idea began to take shape in Miss Pickerell's mind.

"Mr. Humwhistel," she shouted joyfully. "Your molds!"

Mr. Humwhistel looked a little dazed. "My molds?" he asked. "What molds?"

"Why the molds that have been discovered on the moon," Miss Pickerell said. "You told me that—"

"Oh, you mean the mold spores," Mr. Humwhistel corrected her.

"Yes, the mold spores," Miss Pickerell answered, accepting the correction but recollecting very well that it was she who had originally corrected Mr. Humwhistel. "Anyway, you know what I mean."

Mr. Humwhistel seemed a little puzzled.

Miss Pickerell was growing impatient. "Mr. Humwhistel," she said exasperatedly. "Just a few hours ago, you went into a long explanation about the spores that have been discovered on the moon. I remember quite distinctly that you said those spores could be grown into molds."

"Why, yes," Mr. Humwhistel said. "Yes, of course. Our scientists seem to think so."

He looked surprised at Miss Pickerell's renewed interest in the subject.

Miss Pickerell could hardly contain herself. She saw it all so clearly.

"Mr. Humwhistel," she said, talking very slowly and carefully. "Those molds, as you clearly explained to me, may be the means of combating some germ diseases for which modern medicine has not yet found a cure. Such a germ disease has attacked the animals of Square Toe County. It has grown into an epidemic. It must at all costs be stopped!"

Mr. Esticott understood what Miss Pickerell was getting at.

"Good gracious!" he exclaimed.

Mr. Humwhistel understood now, too.

"Are you suggesting," he asked, his voice incredulous, "are you suggesting a trip to the moon to get those spores?"

"I don't see why you sound so amazed," Miss Pickerell said.

Mr. Humwhistel opened his mouth to say something, but Miss Pickerell went right on.

"Do you mean to tell me," she asked. "that you're willing to sit back and do nothing when there is a chance the spores may give us the kind of mold that may provide a cure—"

"But we don't even know if it can provide a cure," Mr. Humwhistel broke in.

"Naturally, we don't," Miss Pickerell said. "No one knew anything about penicillin once. No one really knows anything without trying."

"I agree with you in that respect," Mr. Humwhistel admitted.

"Well, then!" Miss Pickerell said and waited for him to go on.

"It's just that we're not making very regular passenger flights to the moon as yet," Mr. Humwhistel replied apologetically. "The journey there is still experimental in some ways. And, of course, life on the moon, the life of earth people who are stationed there, that is, is still a matter of scientific study."

Miss Pickerell paced back and forth across her big, quiet kitchen.

Mr. Humwhistel looked at her helplessly. "I happen to know," he said, "that the next passenger flight to the moon is reserved for only our most important scientists and that it is not scheduled for another three months. I assure you, Miss Pickerell, that this schedule cannot be changed."

Mr. Esticott sighed. "I'm afraid I have to go now, Miss Pickerell," he said. "It's time for me to relieve Covington."

Mr. Humwhistel mumbled something about needing to go, too.

As he went down the steps of the porch, Mr. Humwhistel turned back once to get a last look at Pumpkins.

Miss Pickerell heard the splutter of the motorcycle starting up, the roar as it charged down her private road, and then a shrill screech of the brakes. She ran to the window just in time to see the motorcycle barely avert a head-on collision with Dr. Haggerty's car. Mr. Humwhistel, who had veered sharply to the left, was now plowing straight through her prize bush of hydrangeas and continuing calmly on his way.

5
Alarming News from Dr. Haggerty

Dr. Haggerty got out of his car without even a backward glance at the motorcycle. He waved to Miss Pickerell as he lifted the latch of the gate and called out for her not to bother to come down and meet him.

"Your cow is resting quietly," he added as soon as he reached the door.

Miss Pickerell could see how hard Dr. Haggerty was trying to smile. She realized he was saying whatever he could to reassure her.

"I want to have another look at Pumpkins," Dr. Haggerty continued.

"Thank you," Miss Pickerell said. "He's been sleeping ever since we left your office."

Pumpkins was still lying on the horsehair

sofa in the hall where Mr. Humwhistel had put him. When Dr. Haggerty and Miss Pickerell approached, he half opened his yellow eyes. Then he closed them again.

"Mercy!" Miss Pickerell exclaimed, listening to the loud sounds Pumpkins was making while he slept. "I believe he's snoring."

Dr. Haggerty bent down to hear the sounds more clearly. He sighed sadly when he looked up again.

"Pumpkins isn't snoring, Miss Pickerell," he said, talking very softly. "It looks very much as though he's having difficulty with his breathing."

Miss Pickerell watched while Dr. Haggerty carefully checked with his stethoscope to make sure.

"Yes," he said, as he replaced the instrument in his little black bag. "The lungs are infected. That's what I was afraid of."

Dr. Haggerty was taking bottles out of his bag. "I'll give him a double antibiotic," he said.

Miss Pickerell remembered what Dr. Haggerty had told her about the way the known antibiotics were not working for this particular disease. She opened her mouth to say something, then closed it again.

Dr. Haggerty understood. He threw out his hands in a small gesture of despair. "We must hope," he said.

Miss Pickerell thought that his voice sounded anything but hopeful. She said nothing.

Pumpkins cried faintly when the needle touched his skin. He seemed too weak even to move. Miss Pickerell shuddered. She simply could not stand it any longer.

"Dr. Haggerty," she said, looking at him resolutely, "may I ask you a few professional questions?"

"Why, yes, Miss Pickerell," Dr. Haggerty replied. "I'm always ready to answer your questions."

Miss Pickerell hesitated for just a minute. She did not like to waste any of Dr. Haggerty's time.

"Dr. Haggerty," she said, "a mold can be grown very simply, can't it? Euphus, my middle nephew, says all you have to do is put the spores in a Petri dish with some kind of solution that nourishes them. Euphus uses a potato in his solutions."

"Agar is more usual," Dr. Haggerty replied, looking a little puzzled because he had not expected this kind of question. "Agar plus salts and proteins."

Miss Pickerell nodded brightly. "Then the next step," she said, going on to her second question, "is to learn whether a mold produces an antibiotic. Is it difficult for scientists to find that out?"

"Not at all," Dr. Haggerty explained. "An antibiotic is any antibacterial or anti-germ substance produced by a living organism. It may be produced by a mold or by some other fungus. All we do is separate this substance from the mold culture, put it in a fresh Petri dish, and add living bacteria. Then we watch for the effect."

"And if the substance destroys the bacteria, we know that it is an antibiotic for that particular germ," Miss Pickerell added. "Is that right, Dr. Haggerty?"

Dr. Haggerty smiled. "That's the general idea," he said. "It's routine now, but it took a lot of scientists to learn the method originally. Some of the antibiotics we have discovered are in very wide use now. We are discovering more every day. But—"

"Dr. Haggerty!" Miss Pickerell exclaimed, interrupting him and talking very fast. "It is possible that a moon mold has been discovered which can produce just the antibiotic we are looking for."

Dr. Haggerty stared at Miss Pickerell.

"Mr. Humwhistel has told me that the scientists in our moon microbiological laboratory have relayed this information to earth," Miss Pickerell continued. "He said specifically that our moon scientists feel very hopeful about its effect on germ diseases we don't know too much about."

"When could we get it?" Dr. Haggerty asked instantly.

Miss Pickerell did not answer him. She had picked up the Square Toe County telephone book and was busy peering intently at its pages over her eyeglasses.

"If it's the right antibiotic," Dr. Haggerty went on, "we could synthesize it, make it from chemicals in a laboratory. That's much quicker than waiting for the molds to grow. We could get vast amounts of the antibiotic, enough for the big animals and the small ones. We could halt the epidemic in a week." He stopped suddenly.

"Pumpkins couldn't wait a week," he said. "He's much too sick."

Dr. Haggerty paused again. "I'm sorry, Miss Pickerell," he apologized, "I didn't really mean to tell you quite so abruptly."

Miss Pickerell looked up from the page she had been examining. "Do you happen to know," she asked Dr. Haggerty, "do you happen to know the name of the man in charge of space flights for this region?"

"Horace T. Blakely," Dr. Haggerty replied promptly. "His official title is Deputy Administrator, Space Traffic Division, Square Toe County, Hog Wallow County, River Bend County, and the Eastern District of Turtle Creek. He's a very important officer."

"That's the man," Miss Pickerell said, making a note of the name and copying the address out of the telephone book. "That's the one I want to see."

"To ask him about getting the spores from the moon?" Dr. Haggerty asked.

"No," Miss Pickerell answered. "To tell him that I can't wait for three months until he sends his next spaceship to the moon."

"But—" Dr. Haggerty asked.

Miss Pickerell looked up at her clock. She put on her apron, poured milk into glasses, and began to spread peanut butter on thick slices of bread for the children she was expecting.

"I must think," Miss Pickerell said. "The children will be here soon. They'll help me keep the disease from spreading. But the most important thing is to get to the moon microbiological laboratory quickly. I'm not giving up. I'll find a way. And I'll tell you another thing, Dr. Haggerty, I'm taking Pumpkins with me!"

6
Mr. Blakely Needs Convincing

Miss Pickerell shook the scarf she was knitting till the needles rattled like castanets and the ball of bright red wool bounded across Deputy Administrator Horace T. Blakely's waiting room. She looked at her watch. It was 10:25. She had been sitting on this hard bench waiting for Mr. Blakely to arrive since exactly five minutes before nine that morning.

A gate outside creaked. Miss Pickerell hastily picked up her ball of wool and put her knitting into her bag. She straightened her hat. The door to the waiting room opened.

"Mr. Blakely? Deputy Administrator

Horace T. Blakely?'' Miss Pickerell asked, looking from one to the other of the two men who entered. One was very tall and wore a uniform. The second had gray hair and carried a briefcase.

"Yes?"

It was the man with the briefcase who answered. He did not smile. Miss Pickerell realized immediately that it was not going to be easy to talk to him. She wasn't at all sure how she ought to begin.

"How do you do, Deputy Administrator Blakely," she said finally, when she saw how the two men stood silently expecting her to say something. "I'm Miss Pickerell. I live on Square Toe Mountain. I have some business I'd like to discuss with you."

Mr. Blakely's eyebrows arched slightly. He waited for her to continue.

Miss Pickerell took a deep breath. She knew she was doing the right thing. She would simply have to try to make him understand. "It's official business," she said as courageously as she could.

The two men exchanged glances. The deputy administrator nodded.

"Please," he said, indicating that Miss

Pickerell was to follow him. He opened a door to his office and politely waited for her to go in. Miss Pickerell saw that the walls of the office were full of charts and astronomers' maps and that there was an engineering mock-up of a space capsule standing near the window. She sat down comfortably in the brown leather armchair across the desk from the deputy administrator.

"I've come about my cow," she said. The minute the words were out of her mouth, she knew she'd said the wrong thing. She could have bitten her tongue. It was too late.

The deputy administrator was looking at her curiously. "Did you say *cow?*" he asked. *"Cow?"*

"I can explain everything, Deputy Administrator," Miss Pickerell began.

"Just call me Mr. Blakely," he interrupted. "And please go on."

"Thank you, Mr. Blakely," Miss Pickerell said, trying to collect her thoughts quickly. "I wouldn't bother you if this weren't an emergency. But I heard from Mr. Humwhistel that the microbiological scientists on the moon—"

"Just a minute, Miss Pickerell," Mr. Blakely interrupted as he turned to the "in" basket on his desk. "I know all about your cow. Mr. Humwhistel telephoned me last night."

He picked up a large manila folder with the words MISS PICKERELL'S COW, CAT, ETC. printed on its oblong label.

"Miss Pickerell," he said, when he had looked through the papers in the folder, "I understand you have been to Mars."

"Yes, Mr. Blakely," Miss Pickerell said. She wondered if the deputy administrator was going to ask her about the red rocks she had brought back from that planet. Almost everybody got around to questioning her about them sooner or later. Miss Pickerell decided to give Mr. Blakely the information as politely and as briefly as she could and to get right back to the subject on her mind.

"Then you know how perilous the journey into space can be," Mr. Blakely went on, not mentioning the rocks after all.

"Yes, I do," Miss Pickerell said quietly.

"It is because we appreciate the dangers, Miss Pickerell," he continued, "that we plan each of our space flights with the utmost care. Mr. Humwhistel has told you, I believe, that we limit our number of scheduled flights and that the priority goes to scientists. Reservations for our next trip were filled at least a year ago.''

"I couldn't wait three months to go on that trip, in any case,'' Miss Pickerell said, feeling desperate and no longer caring how she sounded to the deputy administrator. "If I'm going to save Pumpkins, I have to leave now. I have to get him injected with the new antibiotic before the week is out!''

Mr. Blakely gasped.

"If it's the right antibiotic—'' she added. "But that's a chance I must take.''

Mr. Blakely looked as though he wanted to say something. But he didn't. He simply stared across his desk at Miss Pickerell.

The barking of a dog outside broke the silence. Another dog joined in. All at once, a number of dogs were barking. Mr. Blakely and Miss Pickerell both turned to the window.

A line of dogs was standing just beyond the gate in the yard. The first one carried a stick in his mouth. Attached to the stick was a sign.

At the end of the line stood a girl in a

stiffly starched dress. She held a pink-eared rabbit under one arm and a baby chicken under the other. The girl waved to Miss Pickerell.

"Why, it's Rosemary!" Miss Pickerell exclaimed. "My niece Rosemary! She was at my house last night. I asked her to take as many animals as she could to the doctor. You see, Mr. Blakely, it's an epidemic. But I didn't ask her to bring them here. Why, I never even thought of it. I—"

"Wait," Mr. Blakely said. "Let me talk first. Believe me if I tell you that I fully understand how you feel. But there is noth-

ing I can do. It is impossible to put on an extra emergency ship. As I have already advised you, we need to prepare all space flights very, very carefully. Our planning has to be thorough for both our passenger and cargo efforts. No detail is left—"

Miss Pickerell felt a quick rising surge of hope. "Mr. Blakely," she asked, "did you say something about cargo ships?"

"Certainly," Mr. Blakely answered. "We have cargo spaceships delivering sup-

WE ARE ON OUR WAY TO THE VETERINARIAN WE DONT KNOW IF HE CAN HELP US. CAN YOU?

plies and materials to our base on the moon. The cargo ships also act as mail carriers for the moon post office."

Miss Pickerell was doing some very fast thinking.

"How often do the cargo ships go to the moon?" she asked.

"Once a month," Mr. Blakely replied, proudly pointing to a neatly posted schedule on the wall opposite his desk.

Miss Pickerell was almost afraid to ask the next question. So much depended on it.

"When is the next flight scheduled?" she asked, trying very hard to keep her voice calm.

Mr. Blakely walked over to the wall. "Let me see," he said, as he slid the rubber end of his pencil up and down the schedule of dates. "Ah, here we are. Cargo Spaceship No. 00-41-233, leaving from Square Toe Depot at 2:30 P.M. today."

He moved over to the window. "Perfect weather for the flight," he commented.

Miss Pickerell knew just what she had to do. "Mr. Blakely," she said, "I have an idea. I—"

Mr. Blakely looked at her, the suspicion quickly growing in his eyes. "No," he said, immediately. "No, Miss Pickerell! Absolutely nobody except the crew goes up in a cargo ship!"

"I don't see why—" Miss Pickerell began.

"I'll tell you why," Mr. Blakely interrupted. "I'll tell you why exactly. A trip to the moon is not at all the same as an ordinary airplane flight. In outer space, you have to worry about such things as meteors, sun storms, a disruption of communication with earth, and always, always, uncertain landing conditions."

Miss Pickerell thought he was being extremely illogical. "I know all that," she argued impatiently. "But on a cargo ship it is the same as—"

"On a moon cargo ship," Mr. Blakely went on, "you face all of these ever-present dangers. You also have no room to move around, no upholstered contour couches to soften the impact of take-off and landing, no one with time to stop and talk, and no food except M rations out of a Moon Kit."

Miss Pickerell walked over to where Mr.

Blakely was standing. She held herself very erect when she spoke.

"Deputy Administrator Blakely," she said firmly, "my cow and my cat and a great many other animals in Square Toe County are very, very sick. If you think for one moment that I would let either danger or discomfort stand in the way of any possible chance of my helping them, you don't understand me at all!"

Mr. Blakely did not answer. He stood in front of the window looking straight ahead.

Rosemary had moved down the road with the dogs. Her voice, trying to quiet and reassure them, rose above the faint barks and whimpers.

Mr. Blakely returned to his desk. He took a card out of a drawer, wrote something on it, and rapidly signed his name. "Miss Pickerell," he said, handing the card to her, "your moon cargo-flight authorization! For you and for your Pumpkins!"

7

To the Moon with Pumpkins

Miss Pickerell was nearly shivering with excitement when she got home and began the preparations for her journey. First she called Dr. Haggerty to tell him the news. He said that Rosemary was still in his office. He would send her over by taxi immediately to help with the packing. Rosemary arrived while Miss Pickerell was making out a list of what she planned to take along on the trip.

"We'd better get started right away," Rosemary said, as she looked over the list. "Where's your suitcase?"

Miss Pickerell got her tan satchel out of the closet.

"You won't need much clothing,"

Rosemary suggested. "You'll be wearing a spacesuit."

"Only on take-off and landing," Miss Pickerell corrected her. "In pressurized cabins, you don't need a spacesuit. I'll take my coveralls. And a sweater, in case it gets cold."

"The pink sweater's the prettiest," Rosemary said, taking it out of a drawer and piling it on top of the things she'd already put in the bag.

"And don't forget your knitting," she added, putting that in too. "You'll have plenty of time while you're traveling to finish the fringe on your scarf. I suppose you'll want your umbrella."

"No, there's no rain on the moon," Miss Pickerell said.

The doorbell rang. It was Mr. Humwhistel.

"Mr. Blakely asked me to bring over the spacesuits," he explained. "Pumpkins' may be a little too big for him. It's one of the old ones the space monkeys used."

"I'll put in a few stitches after I get him into it," Miss Pickerell replied.

"Self-sealing stitches," Mr. Humwhistel cautioned.

Rosemary asked whether she should pack Miss Pickerell's diary. And what about some books? And did she want to borrow her camera? Surely, Miss Pickerell would want to take pictures.

Miss Pickerell said to pack the P volume of the encyclopedia and to put the diary into her knitting bag where it would be handy.

"You can wear the camera over your shoulder," Rosemary said. "And I'm packing your navy-blue polka-dot dress, too. It'll be a change from the coveralls."

The doorbell rang again. It was Miss Pickerell's brother, his wife, and Rosemary's six brothers and sisters, who were all shouting at once. Miss Pickerell's brother said that he had come in the big station wagon so that he could drive her and Pumpkins to the space depot. Rosemary reminded Miss Pickerell to take along extra film for the camera. Miss Pickerell looked at the clock and decided it was time for Pumpkins and herself to get into their spacesuits.

The doorbell rang once more. Mr. Esticott entered with a large white bakery box.

"It's for Foster," he explained, "if you

don't mind carrying it. A blueberry upside-
down cake. He has a terrible sweet tooth.
And I don't know just what he's getting to
eat up there on the moon.''

Miss Pickerell went over to the telephone for a last call to Dr. Haggerty. Mr.
Humwhistel said they'd better get moving.
He promised that he'd telephone Dr. Haggerty to ask about the cow regularly. He
would keep Miss Pickerell posted via the
official earth-moon radio network.

Mr. Humwhistel helped Miss Pickerell,
bulky in her spacesuit, into the front seat
of the station wagon. Pumpkins, barely
visible in his oversize monkey's suit, hud-
dled forlornly in her arms. Miss Pickerell's
brother climbed into the driver's seat beside her. Five of the children and their
mother got into the back of the station wagon. Dwight and Rosemary decided to ride
with Mr. Esticott in the car he had bor-
rowed from Covington. Mr. Humwhistel
followed on his motorcycle, tooting all the
way. None of the children ever stopped
talking.

Miss Pickerell had time only to notice
the word *Cow* painted in red on the cargo
ship when they arrived at the depot.

"The ship's named for the cow who jumped over the moon," the crew member who ushered her on board explained. "Here, let me take your bag and your package from you. We have to clamp them down so they don't start floating around once we're coasting in space."

He strapped Miss Pickerell down, too, on the hard, uninviting contour couch which stood wedged between carefully labeled crates of machinery and spare parts on one side and sacks of mail on the other. She heard the roar of the engines and the voice of the crew member shouting to tell her that the cargo spaceship weighed 100,000 pounds, requiring a lot of thrust from the booster rockets before it could go up. Then she felt a mighty force pushing her down on the couch. The rockets fired, and the spacecraft separated itself from the booster and went thundering up into space. Miss Pickerell shut her eyes tight.

When she opened them, the young man who had helped her aboard was suspended in space beside her. Miss Pickerell noticed that he was sunburned and that he had a very nice smile.

"I'm Thurston Williston," he introduced himself, "co-pilot in charge of navigation on this flight. How do you feel, Miss Pickerell?"

"Wonderful," she said. "Anything would be wonderful after all those children. They make almost as much noise as the booster engines on take-off."

"We're up in space now, Miss Pickerell," Mr. Williston said. "You can take off your spacesuit, if you wish. Make yourself comfortable, we have about a 239,000-mile trip ahead. It's going to be sixty hours; perhaps you'd like something to eat."

Miss Pickerell commented that she was too tired to be hungry. "I'll try to give Pumpkins some vitamin snaps, though," she said, opening his helmet.

She reached into the lower right-hand pocket of her spacesuit for the bottle she had packed at the very last minute. Pumpkins sniffed at the two vitamin snaps she held out to him. He ate one of them.

Miss Pickerell thought this was a good sign. She patted him on his head and leaned back on her contour couch. It was made of hard metal and not at all comfortable. But she was very sleepy.

"I'll just take a little nap now," she said,

after she had thanked Mr. Williston. "Just for a few minutes."

Miss Pickerell closed her eyes. She thought of her cow and of how good it would be to have her home again, healthy and happy, her fawn-colored coat shining, her silver bell tinkling, as she grazed peacefully in the pasture. With these thoughts Miss Pickerell fell asleep.

When she awoke, Mr. Williston was floating nearby. In one hand he held a bottle of lemon drink that had a tube sticking out of it and in the other a package of crusty biscuits.

"Better eat something, Miss Pickerell," he said. "According to earth calculations, it's tomorrow. You've slept for fourteen and a half hours."

Miss Pickerell shook her head in disbelief. "I can't imagine why I feel so tired," she said.

"Maybe you'd feel better if you got out of your spacesuit," Mr. Williston suggested.

Miss Pickerell indeed felt very much better when she sat, securely strapped to keep her from floating, in her nice clean coverall and ate from the fiberboard tray

Mr. Williston clamped across her lap. Pumpkins, fastened with a smaller belt to the end of the couch, showed no interest in food. Miss Pickerell wished the trip to the moon didn't have to take so long.

"I'll begin on my diary," she said to herself, taking her pen and the red, plush-covered book out of her knitting bag. "I must be sure to put in how friendly Mr. Williston has been."

She wrote the date very neatly at the right side of the page and tried to think over the events of the last few days. There had been so many, she hardly knew where to begin. She closed her eyes. Doing that sometimes made her think better. Before she knew it, she was fast asleep once more.

When she awoke the second time, she felt completely refreshed. "Mercy!" she exclaimed. "I never thought flying to the moon would be so relaxing. I suppose it's because there's nothing to see outside. Not even clouds."

She unstrapped her belt and floated over to where Mr. Williston sat near a radio-telephone in front of the ship. Two members of the crew, busy checking gauges and instrument readings, cheerfully called out

"Good morning" to her as she passed.

"Excuse me," Miss Pickerell said to Mr. Williston when she had glided up to him. "Can you tell me the time?"

Mr. Williston laughed. "Time is different up in space," he said, "but we'll be approaching Gravity Checkpoint before very long. After that moon gravity begins to pull us down. Did you know that the moon has gravity, Miss Pickerell?"

"Certainly," Miss Pickerell replied. "I know the figures, too. The gravity of the moon is one-sixth of the earth's gravity."

"Bravo!" Mr. Williston exclaimed. "Have some applesauce." He handed over what looked like a giant toothpaste tube.

Miss Pickerell squeezed the applesauce out of the tube and tasted it. It was delicious.

"And what happens after we enter lunar space?" Mr. Williston asked next.

"We check our aim at the moon," Miss Pickerell replied.

"Not *at* the moon," Mr. Williston objected.

"I didn't mean *exactly* at the moon," Miss Pickerell said indignantly. "We can't aim exactly at the moon because the moon

*She floated over to where
Mr. Williston sat.*

doesn't stand still. It moves in its own orbit around the earth.''

She felt very proud as she watched Mr. Williston stare at her in admiration. Then she thought that maybe she was giving an exaggerated impression about her knowledge. She decided that doing this was not very honest.

''I've been reading about it in the encyclopedia,'' she told him. ''The encyclopedia says that the navigator has to aim for a point in space where both the ship and the moon will arrive at the same time. It's explained in detail in the P volume.''

''That's all right, Miss Pickerell,'' Mr. Williston said, smiling. ''I still think you're great.''

Mr. Williston left to go help the captain navigate. Miss Pickerell floated over to the corner where the Moon Kits were fastened down in metal grips and helped herself to a can of chicken hash out of the kit tagged with her name. Then she decided to take her encyclopedia out of her satchel and do some more reading about the moon.

She was just up to the part which told about the huge flat areas known as marias, when the flash signs went into action.

"Don spacesuits!" they signaled in bright red lights. "Test walkie-talkies!"

Miss Pickerell hurried to obey. Then she sat waiting, with Pumpkins in her arms, as the ship descended rapidly and the moon surface came gradually into view. Rugged mountains, steep walls, and craters became larger and larger. Her body felt heavier and heavier. She had a distinct sensation that the ship was falling.

The landing retrorockets were firing.

Everything jolted and shook. Miss Pickerell bounced on her hard contour couch. She held Pumpkins as tightly as she could.

Suddenly, the ship came to a clanging stop. A door opened quickly. A man's voice boomed, "Welcome to Moonport!"

Another man shouted, "Everybody stay aboard! No disembarking until the ship has been sprayed and the Lunar Patrol Officer has checked the ship's manifest!"

Miss Pickerell looked down at Pumpkins, crouched in the spacesuit, his eyes larger than ever in his small, frightened face. "We've arrived, Pumpkins," she said to him gently. "We've arrived where somebody can help you at last!"

8
Welcome to Moonport

"Miss Pickerell!"

A cool, crisp voice called out from the doorway. Two tall, spacesuited figures walked briskly over to her. The first one touched his helmet in a small salute and introduced himself as Base Commander M. M. Manborough. When he stepped aside, Miss Pickerell could see that the other figure was Foster Esticott. Except that his complexion was even ruddier, he looked exactly the same as when she had last seen him on their arctic expedition.

"Why, Foster Esticott," Miss Pickerell exclaimed, "the moon climate certainly seems to agree with you! Your cousin Mr. Esticott was worried about what you were getting to eat up here. He sent you this blueberry upside-down cake." She held up the bakery box.

"I can hardly wait to taste it, Miss Pickerell," Foster said. "I'm glad to see you, but I'm certainly sorry to hear that your cow is sick."

"Mr. Blakely radioed us from earth," Commander Manborough explained. "We'll do all we can for her and your cat. This way out, Miss Pickerell. A moonmobile is waiting to take us to the laboratory." He stepped ahead to open the door for her.

Foster told Miss Pickerell that she looked like a veteran member of the Moon Force in her space helmet. He checked to see that the regulation-size oxygen tank attached to her spacesuit and the smaller one fastened to Pumpkins' were working properly. He picked up Miss Pickerell's satchel and her knitting bag. Miss Pickerell carried Pumpkins and the bakery box with the blueberry upside-down cake.

"We're on our way," Foster said.

Miss Pickerell swung lightly to her feet. "What a wonderful feeling!" she exclaimed, as she stopped for a second to realize what was happening. "With so little gravity, I hardly touch the floor."

She leaped after Foster and Commander Manborough down the short, narrow ladder to the ground. Her throat contracted with excitement when she jumped the last rung and looked around at the awesome world of the moon.

The ship had landed in a layer of shallow dust atop hard rock. Miss Pickerell saw that she was actually standing in the middle of a lunar crater.

"Forevermore!" she breathed.

Foster laughed. "This is only a little crater," he said. "We call it Descartes, after the French mathematician and philosopher. A few of the moon craters go as deep as 20,000 feet and measure more than 100 miles across. Sometimes landing is easier in a crater. Not so much dust."

"Yes," Miss Pickerell said, trying to look everywhere at once.

Jagged cliffs loomed forbiddingly. Towering mountains surrounded her.

Then she saw the sky. The sun was shining, but the sky was black and gleaming with stars. In the distance hung what looked like another moon, big and very, very bright.

"Why, it's the earth!" she exclaimed.

"Want to take a picture?" Foster asked. "It's easy on the moon. No atmospheric troubles to obscure the view. No atmosphere at all!"

Miss Pickerell hesitated. What a wonderful addition this would be to the governor's state science exhibit! She decided against it. There was no time to lose. Pumpkins came first. "Not now, thank you," she said.

"This way to the moonmobile," Foster said, steering her around a large rock to the place where the vehicle was waiting.

Miss Pickerell couldn't make up her mind, when she saw it, whether it resembled a huge caterpillar or some weird sort of tractor. Its body was long and low and mounted on at least a dozen sturdy jeep tires. Four wheels revolved on each axle, for better traction, she supposed. The front and back ends of the moonmobile were flat and open. The middle section, where Commander Manborough sat and where Foster and Miss Pickerell joined him, had a bubbletop hood that enclosed it completely.

"It's a sealed plexiglas cockpit," Commander Manborough said, "for protection against solar radiation and against the meteoroids and temperature extremes on the moon. Some meteoroids are no bigger than dust specks, but they can strike at the rate of sixty a minute."

Miss Pickerell thought back to the conversation she and Mr. Humwhistel and Mr. Esticott had had about air pressure. She knew that the moon had no blanket of air to filter out the sun's fierce heat rays in the day, or to prevent the extreme cooling of its surface at night. The meteoroids were even more frightening.

Foster, ready in the driver's seat, stepped on the gas. The moonmobile pushed across ledges and through crevasses. They passed a mountain range and a number of craterlets. From time to time the stillness was interrupted as meteoroids traveling at tremendous speeds crashed into the plexiglas hood and bounced off. The moonmobile approached a maria. A plaque alongside it announced in several languages that the first lunar landing had been made on this spot, now known as Mare Cognitum or the Sea of Knowledge.

"On that first landing," Commander Manborough said, "a robot spaceship set up the portable reactors for power and communication on the moon."

"Today, we have huge lunar antennas to keep our moon base in touch with the earth," Foster said proudly.

"Slow down a minute," the commander told him. "I want Miss Pickerell to see this." He pointed to a rocket nose, lying half-buried in the dust.

"This was man's first home on the

moon," he said. "The robot ship left it here for him."

Miss Pickerell shuddered to think how difficult life must have been for the first lunarnauts.

"All right," Commander Manborough said. "We'll drive on now, Foster. By earth time, we should be in our lunar colony in just about two seconds."

The moonmobile pushed forward again. Miss Pickerell looked ahead, to the right and to the left. All she could see was a barren, motionless terrain.

"Both our homes and our work areas are underground," the commander explained. "We have learned that for long periods of

time underground installations are more practical. The plexiglas domes of our surface buildings eventually broke under the constant impact of micrometeorites. Also, with our extremes of hot and cold it was too difficult to keep surface buildings at a uniform temperature. You know, it's hard for earth people to live in a place where the temperature can shoot up to 241 degrees Fahrenheit in the middle of the day. That's 29 degrees above the boiling point of water! And it can drop down to 270 degrees below zero Fahrenheit at night. A lunar day and night, that is. Ah, here we are."

Foster pulled up in front of what looked like an entrance to a cave. He got up to help Miss Pickerell out of the moonmobile.

Commander Manborough spoke into his walkie-talkie. "Miss Pickerell and Pumpkins have arrived," he announced.

"We are ready for them," a man's voice answered. "Bring them in."

9
Miss Pickerell Has a Guided Tour

"I know one thing, Dr. Guffey," Miss Pickerell said to the efficient-looking, white-coated young scientist standing near a glass cabinet full of bottles, flasks, and test tubes in the vaultlike microbiological laboratory. "I know that no one is ever going to inject my cat with anything that can possibly do him any harm."

Dr. Guffey shook his head in an impatient gesture. "But I didn't say that, Miss Pickerell," he objected.

He walked over to the straight-backed aluminum bench where Miss Pickerell sat trying to hold a reluctant Pumpkins on her lap. Pumpkins seemed much livelier now that he was no longer wearing his heavy spacesuit. Miss Pickerell wished she had had a few minutes to do more than unstrap her own helmet when they were rushing through the airlock and into the laboratory. She felt awkward and uncomfortable. The bulky gloves clamped to the sleeves of her suit made it difficult to hold on to Pumpkins' fur.

"Miss Pickerell!" Dr. Guffey said. "Please listen to me. What I said was that finding the mold spores was a very important discovery. It meant that there was life on the moon. We may eventually find still other forms of life. The possibilities are enormous!"

Miss Pickerell replied that she couldn't agree more. "But you also said," she reminded him, "that you couldn't be sure about the effect of this antibiotic on Pumpkins."

Dr. Guffey stood up. He took a handkerchief out of his pocket and mopped his forehead. "You know that we have had no chance to test this antibiotic against any great variety of germs, Miss Pickerell," he said. "We can only hope that it will be successful in combating the disease from which your Pumpkins is suffering.''

''Can you tell me just one thing, Dr. Guffey?'' Miss Pickerell asked exasperatedly. ''Can you tell me whether the injection will hurt Pumpkins if it is not the right antibiotic?''

Dr. Guffey looked surprised. ''Oh, you can stop worrying about that, Miss Pickerell,'' he said. ''None of these moon mold antibiotics, whether they are right or wrong for a particular disease, can hurt Pumpkins.''

''In that case—'' Miss Pickerell began. She had no chance to finish. Pumpkins slid off her lap to run and sniff all the exciting odors in this strange new place.

''In that case,'' Dr. Guffey said, bending down quickly and catching Pumpkins up with one long sweep of an arm, ''we'll go ahead. If the antibiotic works, Pumpkins should feel well enough for food in a few hours.''

Dr. Guffey pushed a small buzzer on his desk.

Foster, wearing a dark-blue uniform with gold buttons, entered the laboratory.

''In the meantime,'' Dr. Guffey went

on, "I suggest a tour of our moon colony. Lieutenant Esticott has been waiting to escort you to your room. You might want to have a cup of tea on the way. That will give you a chance to see our new Astral Cafeteria. You will probably want to rest for a while before visiting the other installations."

Miss Pickerell looked at Pumpkins, still squirming in Dr. Guffey's arms. Dr. Guffey waited while she patted Pumpkins reassuringly and promised to return soon. Then Dr. Guffey firmly and politely ushered Foster and Miss Pickerell out of his office.

"I never felt less like resting in my life," Miss Pickerell said, looking up and down the long corridor of closed doors, each with the name and title of its occupant neatly tacked on at eye level. "But I do want to take off my spacesuit."

"You can change in your room," Foster said. "Your satchel's there already. And thank you so much for bringing the cake. It was gone in a few minutes. I shared it with some of the other men on the selenodetic survey. It was the first upside-down cake we've ever had on the moon."

He guided Miss Pickerell around another corridor, then down a sharp ramp to a dim, cavernous entranceway.

"Don't be afraid, Miss Pickerell," he said. "It's only our cross-base tunnel."

Miss Pickerell was just about to tell him that she was not the least bit afraid but that she didn't see why the ramp had to be so steep, when she noticed the tunnel cars. There were six of them, shaped like eggs and suspended from monorails. Each had a different number on the front.

Foster chose the one marked $XX6^27^1G$.

"That's moon language for Apollo Circle, our central working area," he said, as he and Miss Pickerell got in and he pushed a button that whizzed them forward. "It's on our way to the residential quarter. I thought you might want to stop by for a moment."

Miss Pickerell didn't have time to say what she wanted. The car hissed to a stop. She could only gasp at the scene before her. Giant rocket booster tanks, their noses pointing forward, radiated like the spokes of a wheel from what looked like a busy communications hub. Men with earphones and connecting mouthpieces were sitting in

front of radios, facing radar screens lit up
with bouncing waves of light. Other men
sat at machines that reeled out ribbons of
tape with coded messages punched onto
them.

"How long do you think it takes for a
radio signal to get to earth, Miss Pickerell?" Foster asked.

Miss Pickerell thought about this. "That
would depend on the time of the month,"
she said, finally. "It would take less time
when the moon is nearest the earth."

"Good!" Foster applauded. "You certainly know your space science, Miss Pickerell. It takes a radio signal only 1.2 seconds to go from the moon to earth, when
the moon is at perigee."

Miss Pickerell remembered that her
nephew Euphus had once told her about
perigee and apogee. He had said it was
easy to remember which was which because apogee was related to the word apex.
She decided to figure this out a little more
clearly later. She didn't want to miss a
word of the information Foster was giving
her.

"The tapes are a radar transmission system," Foster went on. "We use both radio

and radar to communicate with earth. Eventually, when we have other bases, this communication center will keep all the moon stations in touch with each other."

"Oh!" Miss Pickerell said, visualizing the towns and villages of earth people that might some day be scattered over the moon's craggy surface, and wondering whether the time would ever come when a visit to the moon would be something like going from Square Toe City to the state capital.

"Would you like to take a peek into some of the booster tanks?" Foster asked.

"Please!" Miss Pickerell said, hurrying over to the first one as fast as she could.

"These are our oldest installations," Foster explained, taking rather long strides in order to keep up with her. "Early lunarnaut scientists buried these tanks under moon soil and set them up for working areas. You'll see our modern installations later. We put them farther under—"

"Mercy!" Miss Pickerell interrupted, as she looked into the first booster tank and backed away again.

"It's the lunar processing plant," Foster explained. "Man needs two pounds of oxygen a day to live. We are able to produce 4,000 pounds of liquid oxygen a month from volcanic rock.''

Miss Pickerell did not see how this could be done. She knew that green plants used carbon dioxide for food-making and produced oxygen. But rocks! She turned to discuss this with Foster. He was already telling her about the next tank.

"That's our water conversion installation," he said. "It's set over a furnace from which volcanic rock is mined through a shaft. We extract a gallon of water per cubic foot of rock."

Foster was hurrying on ahead.

"I'm sorry, Miss Pickerell," he apologized. "I just noticed the time on the atomic clock over there. It's later than I realized. I have to get back to my job. We're especially busy these days, finishing up the topography maps of all the small, secondary lunar craters."

Miss Pickerell raced with him, down two more ramps, around a station which he told her was an astronomical observatory where scientists studied different views of the sun, stars, and planets, and down still another ramp.

"Some day, we'll have an elevator," he said breathlessly.

Miss Pickerell replied that she certainly hoped so.

They came to the end of the last ramp. An arrow pointed in the direction of SATELLITE PARK APARTMENTS. A metallic structure, shaped like a Y, spread out before them. It was surrounded by gardens of tiny green plants.

"Duckweed fronds," Foster explained. "To provide lunar food. Also oxygen, we hope. We're experimenting with them."

He handed Miss Pickerell a card that he took out of his pocket. "It's a chart of earth and moon date equivalencies," he said, "in case you want to write some letters. We use a thirteen-month lunar calendar here. Are you sure you'll be all right, Miss Pickerell?"

"Thank you, yes," Miss Pickerell said. "How will I know about Pumpkins?"

"Dr. Guffey will call you on the touchtone telephone," Foster replied. "It's still a long wait, though."

He gave her a key and told her that her room was directly across the hall, through the middle entrance. Miss Pickerell found it easily. There were a number of rooms on the floor. Some had signs on them, saying DO NOT DISTURB.

The first thing she did when she got into her room was take off her spacesuit and change into the polka-dot dress that she took out of her satchel. It made her feel much better. Then she looked around. The room had a side window with only a small view of the gardens, but it had a shower, a luggage rack, a bunk bed, and a chair with an armrest for a desk. The desk had a notice on it announcing the hours when shower water was available, instructions about the button-system telephone, and a map of the Satellite Park installations. Miss Pickerell picked up the map. She saw that the social hall and the medical center were in the left wing of the building. The post office, shopping facilities, and cafeteria were in the right wing. Miss Pickerell was feeling a little hungry. She decided to go and get herself something to eat.

She followed the directions on the map carefully. The Astral Cafeteria was exactly where she thought it would be and, at first glance, looked like an ordinary earth cafeteria. A second look proved that this was

not at all so. The stout man standing behind the counter told her that he could give
her a Galaxy Salad. That proved to be de-
hydrated vegetables in individual portions
in plastic bags. When Miss Pickerell said
that she would take some, the man picked
up a water gun and shot some moisture into
the bag. Then he put the serving on a tray
with a cup of tea. Miss Pickerell tasted the
tea right then and there.

"It has a different flavor, all right," she
said to herself, as she sat down at the first
table. "No wonder, if the water comes
from moon rocks!"

Miss Pickerell was the only one eating
in the cafeteria. She asked the man behind
the counter where everybody was. He said
that he didn't know. He was new on the
moon.

"Moon personnel keep rotating," he
added, "Nobody can stay more than six
months. The artificial atmospheric conditions don't allow it."

Miss Pickerell said that she hadn't had
any difficulty so far. The man said he
hadn't either but he didn't understand too
much about such things. He introduced
himself as Mr. Rugby, and invited Miss

Pickerell to stay on for a few minutes and tell him what she was doing on the moon. Miss Pickerell said that she wished she could but she was on her way to the post office.

In the cubicle post office, she bought a book of Space-Mail moon stamps and asked the attendant where she could get some picture postcards. He directed her to the lunar post exchange next door.

It was a small store and, Miss Pickerell thought, not very orderly. Most of the stock consisted of tools. A young man in baggy overalls was buying what he called a spammer and a plench. He smiled in a friendly way and told her that the spammer was a space hammer, and the plench, a pliers and wrench combination.

The picture postcards hung on a rack in a corner of the post exchange. Miss Pickerell decided that the ones showing man's first footprints on the moon were the most interesting. She bought a package of these.

A number of rocks were displayed on the souvenir counter. Miss Pickerell did not think they were very special but she bought a few for her rock collection. She also chose some moon coins for her nieces'

*The man picked up a water gun and
shot some moisture into the bag.*

charm bracelets and some Space Force insignia, designed with the spider-legged, lunar module in which man originally landed
on the moon, for her nephews.

She was very much surprised to see a
moon newspaper lying near the cash reg-
ister. A small news item, entitled LATEST
BULLETIN, announced her arrival. It said:
"Miss Lavinia Pickerell, from Square Toe
County, U.S.A., arrived on a special mission via spaceship *Cow* early today. At the
moment, Miss Pickerell is the only woman
on the moon." Miss Pickerell bought two
copies.

Back at the Satellite Park Apartments,
she found a note from Foster under her
door. He wrote that he had come during
his work break. He was sorry he had
missed her.

Miss Pickerell wondered how long it
would be before she heard from Dr. Guffey. He had said only a few hours. She
thought of her cow and of poor, sick little
Pumpkins and sighed heavily. She felt suddenly very, very weary. She decided to go
to sleep.

She awoke with a start to the ringing of
the telephone. She rushed to answer it. A

strange voice asked, "Miss Pickerell?"

Miss Pickerell said, "Yes."

"Dr. Guffey wants to speak to you," the voice continued. "Please hang on."

The line became silent. Miss Pickerell waited, her anxiety mounting.

Then Dr. Guffey was on the line. He spoke soothingly. Miss Pickerell knew the news was going to be bad.

"I'm afraid it's the wrong antibiotic, Miss Pickerell," he said, finally. "We can tell without waiting any longer. I thought I'd better tell you. Pumpkins' fever—"

A jangling sound came in on the line. Miss Pickerell could not hear Dr. Guffey.

"What?" she asked. "What did you say about the fever?"

The jangling sound became louder.

"Dr. Guffey! Dr. Guffey!" Miss Pickerell shouted.

There was no answer. The line was dead.

10
Mr. Rugby's Short Cut

Miss Pickerell tried calling Dr. Guffey back immediately. She looked up his number in the three-page moon telephone directory hanging on the doorknob. Then she read the directions for using the touch-tone communications system. All she had to do was push one button after another the way the cashier in the Square Toe City supermarket did on his adding machine. Miss Pickerell pushed the required buttons immediately.

Nothing happened.

She tried again. She also tried calling Foster Esticott, Commander Manborough, the post office, and the lunar post exchange. The keys clicked like little explosions under her frantic fingers. There was no other sound. No buzz or ring came on the line. No voice answered her desperate appeals of "Hello! Hello!"

"I'll just go across the hall and see if a neighbor's phone is working," she resolved. She dressed quickly and buttoned her pink sweater over her coveralls, then made sure that she had her room key in her hand.

Mr. Rugby, looking even stouter than before in his off-duty fatigue uniform, was coming through the entranceway when Miss Pickerell opened her door. He tipped his floppy green hat politely when he saw her.

"How nice to meet you again, Miss Pickerell," Mr. Rugby said. "I've been reading about you in the newspaper."

"Yes," Miss Pickerell replied a bit shortly. She had no time to waste in social conversation.

"Mr. Rugby," she asked, "Do you have a telephone?"

"Of course I have a telephone," he replied immediately. "But haven't you heard? The lines aren't working. The whole cir-

cuit's broken down. It seems to me that
there should be some way of controlling
these accidents. It seems to me that—"

Mr. Rugby went on to give his ideas
about what could be done to make moon
telephone service more reliable. But Miss
Pickerell wasn't listening. She was thinking about the route she had taken with Foster to get to the Satellite Park Apartments
and trying to figure out how she could re-
trace her steps. She broke in on Mr.
Rugby's complaints abruptly.

"Please excuse me, Mr. Rugby," she
said. "Can you tell me exactly how I can
get to the microbiological laboratory? It's
most important for me to get there
quickly."

"I have a map," Mr. Rugby replied
sympathetically. "But I can do better than
that, if you'll permit me, Miss Pickerell. I
can get you to the microbiological laboratory in ten minutes. I know a short cut."

"I'll be ready in less than a minute,"
Miss Pickerell said, as she turned back into
her room. "Wait right here, please, Mr.
Rugby."

Miss Pickerell ran into her room and
snatched up her knitting bag with her hand-

kerchief and extra pair of glasses in it. Then she and Mr. Rugby ran up the first ramp together.

"We go to the left now," Miss Pickerell said, when they reached the top. "I remember—"

"Not if we take the short cut," Mr. Rugby replied, panting a little and removing his hat for an instant so that he could use it as a fan. "Follow me, please."

Miss Pickerell obeyed. Mr. Rugby took her past a huge rocket garage, a cave where liquid hydrogen was stored, and an atomic power plant. He boasted that there were not many earth people who had the chance to see this sort of thing.

It was all very interesting, but Miss Pickerell was sure they were going the wrong way. They had been climbing ramps, racing down inclines, and rushing around unexpected moon installations for a very long time, certainly far longer than the ten minutes Mr. Rugby had promised. He was puffing heavily now.

"Isn't it about time we got to the tunnel?" Miss Pickerell asked. "So that we can catch the monorail car?"

"We don't catch the monorail car," Mr.

Rugby replied. "Not with the short cut."

Miss Pickerell gritted her teeth. Mr. Rugby seemed to know as little about the underground passages of the moon as she did. She had a good mind to tell him so. Before she could think of a polite way to express her opinion, however, Mr. Rugby had taken her up another ramp, through a small tunnel, and out into a lighted hallway. Miss Pickerell recognized it instantly. It was the back way to the microbiological laboratory. She nearly laughed out loud with relief.

"Thank you," she said to Mr. Rugby. "Thank you very much. I know exactly where I am now."

She hurried to find Dr. Guffey's office. The sign on his door said KNOCK AND ENTER. Miss Pickerell did so.

Dr. Guffey was sitting at his desk. He looked up at her briefly from some papers he was studying. "Ah, Miss Pickerell," he said. "I'm sorry we were disconnected. I was trying to tell you that Pumpkins' fever was still the same. He did not respond to the antibiotic. I'm afraid there's nothing more we can do."

Dr. Guffey walked quickly into another

room and came back with a small animal carrier which he put on his desk. Through the tiny screened window, Miss Pickerell could see Pumpkins' yellow eyes looking out at her. He meowed weakly.

"Dr. Guffey—" Miss Pickerell began.

"The monkey suit is in the carrier," Dr. Guffey went on. "You will probably want to make some arrangements about getting back to earth. It is possible that the cargo ship you came on has not returned as yet."

"Dr. Guffey—" Miss Pickerell began again.

"Commander Manborough is the person to get in touch with about that," Dr. Guffey continued. "Let me just see if the line's been repaired."

He turned to try the telephone on his desk.

"Dr. Guffey!" Miss Pickerell said, as loudly as she could. "I want to ask you a question."

"Yes, Miss Pickerell?" Dr. Guffey said, turning back to her.

"Dr. Guffey," Miss Pickerell said, "didn't you say that finding these mold spores could mean that there were other forms of life on the moon?"

"We certainly hope so, Miss Pickerell," Dr. Guffey replied. "We have been searching almost inch by inch. By this time, we have covered nearly the entire surface of the near side of the moon."

Miss Pickerell stared at him. "Did you say the near side of the moon, Dr. Guffey?" she asked.

Dr. Guffey shrugged his shoulders. "We call it that," he said. "You see, the moon rotates on its axis at the same time that it revolves around the earth. It makes one spin for each of its revolutions. As a result, the moon always keeps the same side to the earth."

He moved toward the telephone. "I'll see if I can reach—" he said.

"Dr. Guffey!" Miss Pickerell shouted, stopping him short once more. "What about the far side of the moon?"

Dr. Guffey looked puzzled. "What about it?" he asked.

"Has anyone looked to see if there are any forms of life on that side of the moon?" Miss Pickerell wanted to know.

"Not yet," Dr. Guffey said.

"I don't see why not," Miss Pickerell said. "For all we know, there may be mold spores on the far side of the moon."

Dr. Guffey picked up the animal carrier from his desk and handed it to Miss Pickerell. Pumpkins' small black paw was against the little window now. He was clawing the screen in an effort to get out.

"Good-by, Miss Pickerell," Dr. Guffey said. "You have some very good ideas. Perhaps some day we'll be able to carry them out. A study of the surface of the other side of the moon is, unfortunately, not on our current schedule. I'll ring for someone to accompany you back to your room. And I'll be in touch with Commander Manborough about possible cargo spaceship passage."

"I'm not taking the cargo ship," Miss Pickerell announced.

Dr. Guffey looked at her questioningly.

"No," Miss Pickerell said with unmistakable decision. "As long as there is even the remotest chance of saving Pumpkins or my cow or any of the other sick animals, I must keep on trying. If you won't go and look at the soil on the far side of the moon, I'll have to do it myself."

the corridor only to r

11
Off to the Far Side of the Moon

Standing outside Dr. Guffey's door in the lonely moon corridor, Miss Pickerell nervously considered whether she could really carry out her intention. To begin with, she knew nothing about lunar soil examination. But, then, digging was only digging, after all, she reasoned. And if she could just get a few samples of the soil on the other side of the moon and have them analyzed, she would at least feel that she had tried.

Pumpkins meowed again. Miss Pickerell talked to him through the little screened window. "Don't worry, Pumpkins," she said. "We'll find a way. First, we'll go back to the room."

She started walking toward the end of the corridor, only to meet Foster running up the ramp that led from the cross-base tunnel.

"Miss Pickerell!" he said breathlessly. "What's the matter? Dr. Guffey telephoned. Commander Manborough, too. They said to come and help you get ready to go back to earth."

"Foster," Miss Pickerell asked, "have you ever been to the far side of the moon?"

Foster nodded and held up two fingers to show how many times. He was still trying to catch his breath.

"How did you get there?" Miss Pickerell asked.

"Our moon-mapping ship," Foster said. "It's a small rocket-probe craft."

"Good!" Miss Pickerell said, approvingly. "That settles it."

"Settles what?" Foster asked. "I'm sorry, Miss Pickerell. Nobody told me anything."

"I'll tell you," Miss Pickerell said. "I'm using that ship to go to the far side of the moon. I'm going to dig up samples of soil from as many places as possible."

"Who has been assigned to work with you, Miss Pickerell?" Foster asked. "Soil sampling is a complicated process."

"Oh, pooh!" Miss Pickerell said. "Anybody can dig a hole!"

"Not on the moon," Foster insisted, "not without a heavy shovel in the places where the dust is packed solid. For all I know, the dust may be thick practically everywhere on the far side of the moon."

Miss Pickerell remembered the hardware section in the lunar post exchange.

"I'll get a shovel," she told Foster. "In the post exchange. I have to go back for my spacesuit anyway. How much time will we need for you to take me there?"

Foster looked at her helplessly. "I guess I could get you there in a little over an hour. But I ought to have written orders and—"

"You don't understand," Miss Pickerell burst out. "This is an emergency. The antibiotic Dr. Guffey tried out on Pumpkins was still not the right one. We must try the far side of the moon to see if there are other mold spores."

"Well, you certainly know how to cut red tape quickly," Foster said, though he still looked uneasy.

Miss Pickerell watched him expectantly.

"If we're going, we'd better get started

right away," Foster announced finally. "There was some talk at the laboratory about solar noises. That's the sound we hear when a sun storm is coming. We get static or crackling over the radio. Probably nothing to get alarmed about."

"I'll go get my spacesuit," Miss Pickerell said. "And the shovel."

Foster said that wouldn't be necessary. They could get everything they needed in the supply room next to the airlock.

"Mr. Rugby will help you find a suit in your size," he said, steering Miss Pickerell in the direction of the exit that led to the moon's surface.

"Mr. Rugby!" Miss Pickerell exclaimed. "That's the man in the cafeteria."

"He works in the supply room, too," Foster said. "Part time. He says he gets lonely when he's not working."

Mr. Rugby smiled broadly when he saw them approaching. He helped Miss Pickerell and Foster get into their bulky spacesuits and adjusted their walkie-talkies. He gave each of them two oxygen packs, one strapped across the back and one against the thigh.

"Each pack contains enough oxygen for twenty minutes on the moon," Foster explained.

"If we move quickly from place to place," Miss Pickerell said, thinking out loud, "we can collect quite a few samples of moon soil in forty minutes."

Mr. Rugby nodded his agreement. "You might also want to take a few pictures," he recommended.

Miss Pickerell already had her gloves on. She asked Mr. Rugby if he would mind getting her camera out of her knitting bag. Mr. Rugby found it under her diary and put it into the pocket of her spacesuit. He promised to take good care of both her knitting bag and the animal in the carrier for her until she returned.

"But I'm taking Pumpkins with me!" Miss Pickerell exclaimed in a horrified tone of voice. "I wouldn't think of going without Pumpkins!"

Mr. Rugby looked hurt.

"It has nothing to do with you," Miss Pickerell told him. "I just can't bear the thought of leaving Pumpkins behind."

Mr. Rugby said that he understood. He

dressed Pumpkins in his monkey spacesuit and attached a small extra oxygen tank to the suit.

Foster asked for two shovels. Then he checked to see that all the oxygen packs were securely connected to their openings in the spacesuits.

"Ready to go, Miss Pickerell?" he asked, when he was sure that everything was in order.

"Ready!" Miss Pickerell replied.

They stepped into the airlock together. Foster closed the door tightly behind them. An automatic valve swished into action. The air pressure was changing.

Miss Pickerell stood next to Foster, waiting. She knew that the outer door would open only when the pressure in the airlock was the same as the pressure outside. Later, when the door closed behind them, the pressure would change back again. That was how the earth people kept a steady atmosphere inside the base, she supposed, by locking up the inside air.

The swishing noise stopped. The door opened. Miss Pickerell followed Foster out on the surface of the moon.

Her eyes were dazzled by the natural light of the sun. Living under the artificial, underground lights, she had almost forgotten how bright the sun could be. It was shining now with a hard, intense glare.

"How hot is it?" Miss Pickerell asked Foster through her walkie-talkie, as she skipped lightly beside him in her almost weightless state.

Foster replied that he didn't know exactly. But it hardly mattered. Their spacesuits were temperature-controlled.

He walked quickly to what Miss Pickerell saw was a small landing field. A number of sausagelike vehicles were parked on ring-shaped, elevated platforms. The ships stood straight up like small rockets.

They climbed up a rope ladder past the platform, all the way up to the nose. Foster helped Miss Pickerell crawl inside the cockpit. Then he pulled in the ladder. He carefully tied down the two shovels in a lower compartment next to the fuel tanks. He and Miss Pickerell strapped themselves into their seats. Miss Pickerell fastened Pumpkins, who was sleeping now, across her lap. Foster plugged the line from his earphones into the ship's radio and motioned to Miss Pickerell to do the same. He spoke to the control tower.

"Rocketcraft No. 12-12-22," he announced. "Taking off from landing field Diana. Destination: far side of the moon. Mission: exploratory survey. Lieutenant Foster Esticott piloting."

"12-12-22, I don't find you on the schedule," a voice from the tower answered.

"Emergency for microbio. lab. Short trip to pick up samples," Foster replied.

"Roger. Proceed on course. I've listed your return for approximately two and one-half hours from now," the tower said.

Foster pressed some buttons on his instrument panel. Launching rockets responded immediately. The rocket-probe craft rose directly skyward, teetered slightly, and then moved forward.

Only then did Foster realize that Miss Pickerell was frantically trying to get his attention. He clicked a switch that turned off the radio and allowed him to speak to Miss Pickerell through the walkie-talkies they wore.

"Now we can relax," he said to her.

"The base will guide us by radar. We just follow the beam."

"Foster, I'm afraid you've misunderstood," Miss Pickerell said slowly. "I mean about the flight and schedule. This trip has been entirely my responsibility, I'll explain that to Commander Manborough."

"Miss Pickerell," Foster gasped, "you don't mean that no one authorized the trip? Didn't you tell me Dr. Guffey had sent you to me?"

"No, I was simply telling you that this was an emergency and the microbiological laboratory needed more samples," Miss Pickerell replied.

Foster groaned. "Miss Pickerell, they'll probably ship me back to earth on the next cargo flight," he said.

"Mercy! I'd never forgive myself," Miss Pickerell exclaimed. "Must we go back?"

"We're listed for return in two and a half hours. Better not complicate the schedule any further. Maybe if we find some spores, the trouble won't be quite so bad," Foster said in a resigned tone.

He was leveling off the ship a little and calculating its position according to the ra-

dar beam. "We make a wide turn to the far side of the moon now," he said.

After a while, Miss Pickerell looked out at the moonscape below. The surface of the far side of the moon appeared almost the same as it did on the near side. Rocks, cliffs, dust, loneliness. Nothing else.

She leaned over to see how Pumpkins was doing. He was awake now and stirring restlessly in the spacesuit. She hoped as hard as she could that she would be able to help him. She wondered why Mr. Humwhistel hadn't gotten in touch with her about her cow. He had promised to keep her informed. Perhaps he had tried and she hadn't been there to get the message. She asked Foster about this.

"I can find out," Foster offered. "I'll call the lunar base."

He switched on the radio again. A stream of jarring, spluttering noises came through the earphones. They were so loud, Miss Pickerell reached up to cover her ears, then realized she had a space helmet on.

"Static," Foster said, turning the set off again.

"The sun storm!" Miss Pickerell exclaimed, remembering what Foster had told her.

"Probably," Foster replied. "But don't worry, we have them all the time."

"Goodness!" Miss Pickerell said.

"The sun is never quiet," Foster went on. "It's always ejecting thousands of tons of matter in all directions. They're only tiny bits of matter, though, blowing around in what we call a solar wind."

Foster tried the radio again. It was still spitting static. He consulted the radar beam.

"We're aiming for one of the marias," he told Miss Pickerell. "It's a good landing site."

His voice sounded anxious. He was watching the radar beam again. Miss Pickerell looked with him. The lights seemed very faint.

"Is anything wrong, Foster?" Miss Pickerell asked.

"Not really," Foster said. "It could be that this is going to be a solar flare. That's a giant sun storm, with millions of bits of matter whirling around. But it's not very likely."

He and Miss Pickerell looked out at the terrain before them. Nothing was moving.

"Wherever that storm is, it's having an effect on us," Foster muttered. He was leaning over the radar beam now, trying to make out the green lights that were becoming more and more indistinct.

"I'm afraid the radar's going," Foster said, just as the screen went blank. "I don't know where we are. I can't get my position. We'll have to land right now."

"You mean a crash landing?" Miss Pickerell asked anxiously.

"Not exactly," Foster said. "We'll just

land in an avalanche of dust. Be sure your seat belt's on tight, Miss Pickerell. We're going down now.''

12
Lost in a Sun Storm

"Mercy!" Miss Pickerell exclaimed when the retrorocket motors had stopped their firing and the ship had come to rest in a furious scattering of dust.

"We'll have to jump for it," Foster shouted through his walkie-talkie. "This way, Miss Pickerell!"

He steered her rapidly out of the cockpit. Before she had more than a chance to tighten her hold on Pumpkins, Foster had clutched her around the waist and lifted her with him in a jump to the edge of a shallow crater.

"Mercy!" Miss Pickerell said again,

when they were on their feet once more. "I never knew jumping could be so easy. But I suppose it's the gravity. Or rather, the near lack of it."

They turned around to look at the ship. It had anchored itself in a tilting position against a crater wall. Dust was pouring down from all sides. The ship was already submerged in what seemed to be mountains of dust almost covering its plexiglas nose. The shovels were buried deep inside.

"What do we do now?" Miss Pickerell asked in an awe-struck voice.

"We wait," Foster said. "The base is bound to track us down. They'll send a rescue ship."

Miss Pickerell tried to push the thought out of her head, but she could not help remembering about the oxygen packs. Forty minutes was the limit that she, Foster, and Pumpkins could remain on the moon's surface and survive.

"I've brought you into all this danger," Miss Pickerell said to Foster. "I can't tell you how sorry I am."

"The rescue ship is probably on its way already," he said reassuringly. "They realized at the base the minute we lost contact that something was wrong. I'm sure they sent out a ship immediately.''

Miss Pickerell looked down at the ground. She didn't want Foster to see the doubt in her eyes. He seemed to have forgotten that their radar system was no longer working. How could the rescue ship even know where to begin to look for them?

''These solar outbursts rarely last long,'' Foster went on. ''Anyway, it's only the solar noises that interfere with communication. Once those die down, the base will be able to home into our rocket ship's radar. The beacon we have there is automatic.''

''I see,'' Miss Pickerell said, trying hard to understand. The way Foster explained it, the radar beacon in the probe ship would start sending signals again as soon as the worst of the storm was over. It sounded encouraging.

She thought of taking a look around while they were waiting. In all likelihood, she would never have a chance to be on the far side of the moon again. And seeing the sights might take her mind off her fears. She proposed the idea to Foster.

"Just don't walk too far," he warned her. "These are low-frequency walkie-talkies. They won't operate beyond a certain point."

"I'll just go a little way," Miss Pickerell assured him.

She transferred Pumpkins from one arm to the other. He was completely awake now and staring at her curiously out of his spacesuit. She couldn't think of anything comforting to say to him.

The moon looked bleak and desolate. Miss Pickerell scuffed the ground as she went along. It was solid and the dust was pretty thick. Without a shovel or maybe even a drill, there didn't seem to be a chance in the world of getting into it.

Pumpkins meowed. Miss Pickerell put him back on her other arm.

Foster's voice sounded on her walkie-talkie. "Don't go too far," he reminded her.

"I won't," Miss Pickerell called back into her mouthpiece microphone.

She turned around and waved to him.

Walking on the moon was so easy. If she didn't watch herself, she would be running without even knowing it. She tried to slow down to a kind of shuffle, dragging her feet along the dust as she walked. In some places, it was definitely looser than in others. One spot she stepped on seemed to give way rather easily. She leaned down to examine it more closely. She forgot about holding on to Pumpkins tightly. He leaped from her arm to the ground.

"Pumpkins!" Miss Pickerell shouted, reaching out after him.

Startled by her gesture, he looked up at her. Then he ran. Miss Pickerell ran after him.

"Pumpkins! Pumpkins, please stop!" she called, forgetting that he could not hear her voice on the moon.

Pumpkins ran right on. He seemed enchanted by his sudden freedom in this great, big place where his spacesuit weighed almost nothing. He sprinted easily over two small rocks, landed lightly on a patch of ground, and began to dig violently.

Miss Pickerell watched open-mouthed. Pumpkins was moving layer after layer of dust with his two front paws. The heavy space mittens he was wearing didn't even seem to be in his way. He was actually pushing soil out from under the dust and letting it pile up in little heaps around a tiny hole he was making.

"Forevermore!" Miss Pickerell whispered.

She moved cautiously toward him. If she frightened him, he would run again.

But Pumpkins was too intent on his digging to care about what Miss Pickerell was doing. She jumped quickly over the two rocks that separated them and leaned down

and grabbed him. For one terrifying second, she thought he was about to slide out of her grasp. But she took a firmer hold and got him under her arm.

"Pumpkins! Pumpkins!" she said, over and over again, hugging him and nearly crying with relief. She had been so close to losing him.

Then she thought of the soil. The bits that lay deep in the hole looked darker and richer than the rest. If there were mold spores anywhere, they could be in this moon soil that Pumpkins had dug up from under the layers of dust. It seemed reason-

able to think so because soil was not exposed to such great temperature extremes down there. She began frantically to gather the soil into a pocket of her spacesuit.

It was a difficult task. She could use only one hand. She did not dare to release her hold on Pumpkins. And gathering soil with a space glove on was harder than digging. But she persisted. She picked up handful after handful until the pocket was full. Then she pulled the zipper up and locked it securely.

"The spores are all mixed up with the soil," she said, as she straightened up. "But surely, they'll know at the laboratory how to separate all that."

She hugged Pumpkins again and turned to go back to the ship. "I guess I've lost my bearings," Miss Pickerell said. "It must be in the other direction."

She turned again. She moved slowly to the right in a complete circle. Then she reversed herself and turned slowly to the left. She did not know what to make of it. Foster was nowhere in sight.

13

Flash to the Rescue Ship

Miss Pickerell was panicky for only a moment. She knew she could speak to Foster even if she didn't see him.

"Yoo hoo," she called through her walkie-talkie. "Foster! Where are you?"

"Right here, Miss Pickerell," Foster's voice came back. "Near our ship, where you left me. Where are you?"

"I don't know," Miss Pickerell answered. "I can't see you. I've looked in every direction."

The walkie-talkie was quiet for a long, frightening minute. At last, Foster spoke again. "Miss Pickerell," he said. "Listen carefully!"

"Yes, Foster," she replied.

"Do you remember that Mr. Rugby put your camera in the pocket of your space-suit?"

"Of course, I remember," Miss Pickerell said.

"O.K.," Foster said. "I have an idea what your camera looks like. We'll use the electronic flash as a signal. That's the part that automatically lights up when you snap a picture. It works on a battery. Have you ever used it, Miss Pickerell?"

"No," Miss Pickerell said meekly. "Not yet."

"Don't worry," Foster assured her. "It's easy. Take the camera out of your pocket now, will you, Miss Pickerell? Let me know when you have it in your hand."

Miss Pickerell fumbled with the left-hand pocket of her spacesuit. She got it open finally and pulled the camera out. "I have it, Foster," she announced.

"Good," he said. "Hold it up in front of you. There's a switch marked STROBE LIGHT just above the lens opening. Make sure that's on. Now find the button on the right side. That's the picture-snapping button. With the strobe switch on, you get a flash when you push the button. Keep turning in a slow circle and press every three seconds. Keep pressing until I tell you to stop. Can you manage, Miss Pickerell?"

"Yes," she said, hopefully.

The camera just about fitted into the palm of her hand. She separated her gloved fingers so that she could push the button with her forefinger. She made sure that her hold on Pumpkins in her other arm was absolutely secure. Then she lifted the camera, aimed it so that the shutter faced front, and began to turn slowly.

She counted the seconds by saying each numeral out loud and whispering the word "pause" between them. This kept her from going too fast.

"One, pause; two, pause; three, pause." After every third count, she pressed the button.

Then she counted again: "One, pause; two, pause; three, pause."

"Stop!" Foster's voice commanded. "Stay where you are! Don't move, Miss Pickerell."

Miss Pickerell obeyed instantly. "I've stopped, Foster," she told him.

"Fine," Foster replied. "I can see you

now, Miss Pickerell, and I'm coming toward you. Stand still and flash every seven seconds."

"Every seven seconds," Miss Pickerell repeated, and began to count again.

"Fine! Fine!" Foster called each time she pushed the button. "I see your light."

She wished he would come soon. Her arm was getting tired from being held in one position for so long. The space gloves were so thick that she couldn't be sure how firmly she was holding the camera. She took her eyes off the button to take a fast look around for Foster.

He was walking toward her, his eyes concentrated on the small, blinking light of her camera. She could also see, flying above in the dark, cloudless sky, the unmistakable silver gleam of a rocket ship. It was passing over Foster, away from the direction he was taking to reach her. She knew what had happened. The pilot hadn't seen them. He was going on to search for them near the probe craft, and they were not there!

Miss Pickerell acted quickly. As soon as the thought came into her head, she knew what to do. She turned the palm of her hand so that it was parallel to the sky. The lens of the camera now faced the rescue ship. She pushed the button. Once, twice, three times, four times . . .

A new voice sounded on the walkie-talkie. "We see your lights," it said. "We see your lights. Rescue ship descending. Rescue ship descending."

Foster touched her sleeve. He was standing beside her.

"You did it, Miss Pickerell!" he said excitedly. "You did exactly the right thing."

Miss Pickerell breathed a deep sigh of relief.

The spaceship approached. It zoomed upward and maneuvered until it was almost directly above them. Miss Pickerell saw the bursts of flame and vapor as the descent engines fired and the ship gently dropped straight down to a vertical position on a patch of hard, crusted ground.

She and Foster waited just long enough for the engines to be cut off. Then they ran quickly to the rescue ship.

Its plexiglas nose was open by the time

they got there. A spacesuited figure waved to them. His voice sounded on the walkie-talkie.

"Hello, Miss Pickerell," he said. "Are you all right?"

There was no mistaking those cool, crisp tones. "I'm fine, Commander," she replied immediately.

"Lieutenant Esticott," Commander Manborough went on. "What about you?"

"In good shape, sir," Foster replied.

"We're throwing down the rope ladder," the commander announced. "Come aboard quickly. Would you like Major Finch to come down and help you, Miss Pickerell?"

Another spacesuited figure, a rolled ladder in his hands, appeared beside the commander.

"No, thank you, Commander," Miss Pickerell replied.

"The ladder is weighted," Major Finch said. "There's nothing to be afraid of. Just get a firm grip."

He pitched the ladder out of the cockpit. It fell into place against the side of the ship.

Miss Pickerell looked up to where Major Finch was standing. The distance between them was at least twenty-five feet. This ship seemed much larger than Foster's moon-mapping craft. Miss Pickerell was sure of it when she noticed *Mooncraft No. 1,* painted in red below the cockpit, and right next to the Space Force insignia, the name MANBOROUGH. It was the commander's own ship. She simply had to be brave to show him how grateful she was.

"Would you like me to hold Pumpkins for you?" Foster asked.

"I'll manage, Foster, thank you," Miss Pickerell said, resolutely tightening her fingers around Pumpkins who lay cradled in her left arm and slinging the strap of her camera over her right arm. With her free right hand, she held on to one side of the ladder.

The voices chimed into her walkie-talkie as she took her first step.

"Easy now," Commander Manborough said.

"Keep looking up. Up only!" Major Finch warned.

"I'm right behind you," Foster reassured her.

In no time at all she was up, and Commander Manborough and Major Finch were reaching out to help her through the hatchway. Foster followed her quickly.

"Welcome aboard!" Commander Manborough said, resealing the hatch. Major Finch fastened Miss Pickerell onto a reclining seat behind Commander Manborough. Foster sat on another reclining seat directly in back of Major Finch.

Commander Manborough took a quick glance around to make sure that everything was under control. "Let's get going," he said to Major Finch.

"Yes, sir," Major Finch replied.

"Miss Pickerell," Commander Manborough said sternly, "we are glad to have you back, but you realize of course that pirating a rocket ship and its pilot is just as unlawful on the moon as it is on earth! And you, Lieutenant Esticott, will have a lot of explaining to do."

"It was my fault, Commander," Miss Pickerell said. "Please don't blame Foster. When I told him we had to make an emergency trip for more spore samples, he thought that you and Dr. Guffey were sending me. I'm very sorry."

Not really feeling too sorry, Miss Pickerell patted her pocket full of moon soil and looked happily down at Pumpkins.

"And now let's hurry to the laboratory," she called to Major Finch. "To the microbiological laboratory!"

14
Will Miss Pickerell
Make History?

"What did you say about the microbiological laboratory?" Commander Manborough asked when he had switched off the relaunching rockets, reported the safe rescue over the radio, and swung the ship around on a course toward the base.

Miss Pickerell realized with a start that she hadn't had a chance to tell even Foster about the moon soil she had gathered.

"I have it right here in my pocket," she said, trying to explain everything at once. "The dark soil that Pumpkins dug up. When he ran away from me for just a minute. That's how I got lost, running after him."

Commander Manborough gulped twice. Miss Pickerell could hear the sound clearly over her walkie-talkie.

"Let's start at the beginning," he said. "Are you trying to tell me, Miss Pickerell, that Pumpkins got beneath the dust into the moon soil?"

"It was a place where the dust was not very solid," Miss Pickerell admitted. "And cats can dig faster than we can."

"I suppose they can," Commander Manborough agreed. "In our own explorations on the near side, we haven't found the digging any too easy."

Miss Pickerell felt very proud.

"Miss Pickerell!" Commander Manborough said suddenly. "This soil that you and Pumpkins managed to gather may be far more important than you realize."

"If you mean that it may contain the mold that will help Pumpkins, Commander," Miss Pickerell said, "I—"

"I don't know what it may contain," Commander Manborough broke in. "But I'm giving orders to prepare for its immediate examination."

He switched the button that connected him with the base communications center.

"Manborough talking," he announced. "Returning with first samples of soil from far side of moon. Notify microbiological laboratory and all other installations concerned."

"Roger!"

Miss Pickerell heard the immediate response in her earphones. Major Finch had plugged in her line to a side radio panel. Listening over the ship's radio reminded her of Foster's earlier effort to contact the base. She still did not know whether there was any message from Mr. Humwhistel about her cow. No message could mean that the news was bad and that Mr. Humwhistel hadn't wanted to tell her. Miss Pickerell resolutely pushed this terrible thought out of her head. She made up her mind to check personally as soon as she got back to the base.

She sat up as straight as she could in her tilted chair and turned to Foster. "Dr. Guffey will be very much surprised when we bring back the soil sample," she said.

"Every laboratory on the moon is going to want to analyze it," Foster replied. "For mineral content, for radioactivity—"

"Base to *Mooncraft No. 1,*" the voice

coming through the radio cut in. "Microbiological laboratory reports nutrient solution for soil sample being prepared. Lab standing by to observe possible presence of organisms."

Miss Pickerell knew what that meant. If they found spores in her moon soil, they would have to grow them into a mold—in a good, nourishing solution, with plenty of warmth, the way her nephew Euphus did it. But then they would have to learn whether the mold produced an antibiotic substance, and, after that, whether it was the right antibiotic for Pumpkins. She sighed with impatience.

Miss Pickerell looked out at the deep, black sky. The stars and planets were shining with an unchanging, electric brilliance. She wondered why she had not noticed before that they shone in different colors. They were green and orange and various shades of blue.

"How beautiful!" she whispered.

"Before you go back to earth, you must come and visit our astronomical observatory," Commander Manborough suggested. "You'll be able to see the nine planets of the sun and, in between Mars and Jupiter, you'll see thousands of little planets or asteroids, revolving right around with them. On the moon you need only a small telescope to see them clearly."

"I'd love to come, Commander," Miss Pickerell said. "Thank you."

"We're making a special study of the planet Venus now," Commander Manborough went on. "It's the brightest planet we can see. Its surface is covered by masses of clouds, though."

Miss Pickerell scanned the sky to see if from this view she could differentiate between the planets and the stars. "Is that a star?" she asked Foster, pointing to a glint of light which suddenly seemed very near.

"Oh, no!" Foster exclaimed. "That's our communications satellite. That's the relay that wasn't relaying when our radar and radio got knocked out before. The telephones, too."

The ship was going down now in a new burst of rockets. It descended quickly and easily to its vertical position on the Diana landing field. Commander Manborough got out first and helped Miss Pickerell down the ladder to the surface. Foster and Major Finch followed.

Miss Pickerell turned to thank Commander Manborough. Then, clutching Pumpkins tightly, she began running in the direction of the microbiological laboratory. "I know the way," she assured Foster.

It wasn't until she was at the entrance to the airlock that she noticed Commander Manborough beside her.

"I'm going with you, Miss Pickerell," he said, just before the door slid open. "If history is being made today, I want to be there to see it."

15

The Right Antibiotic

It was Commander Manborough who gave Miss Pickerell the first news about the spores. He nearly fell over her when he rushed out of Dr. Guffey's office into the long, narrow corridor.

"Excuse me," he said automatically, as he side-stepped the folding stool she was sitting on. Then he looked down and saw her. "Why, Miss Pickerell!" he exclaimed. "I thought you would be visiting the mineralogical collection while you were waiting."

"Thank you, I've been there, and to the astronomical observatory, too," Miss Pickerell replied curtly. "Is there any news, Commander?"

Commander Manborough stared at her in amazement. "Hasn't anybody told you,

Miss Pickerell?'' he asked. ''Oh, yes, Dr. Guffey was trying to telephone you. Your soil was full of spores. We've just sent another expedition out to search for more samples. There's no telling what we'll find!''

''And Pumpkins?'' Miss Pickerell asked anxiously.

Commander Manborough looked apologetic. ''I'm sorry, Miss Pickerell,'' he said. ''I should have told you this first. Dr. Guffey used special heat lamps to grow the mold quickly.''

''Did he find an antibiotic?'' Miss Pickerell burst out.

''We can't rush things,'' Commander Manborough warned. ''Dr. Guffey discovered what he considers a most interesting antibiotic substance. And he has already injected Pumpkins. But we must remember, Miss Pickerell, Pumpkins was given a moon mold antibiotic injection once before. We have to wait again and hope.''

Miss Pickerell sighed wearily. ''I wish it were tomorrow,'' she said.

''You won't have to wait that long,'' Commander Manborough said cheerfully. ''In the meantime, let me extend to you

Dr. Guffey's congratulations, Miss Pickerell. Mine, too, of course. We are greatly indebted to you for your perseverance, your courage, and your—"

Mr. Rugby came running up.

"Oh!" Miss Pickerell exclaimed. "Did you ask about—"

"Beg pardon, sir," Mr. Rugby said, saluting. "I'm sorry to interrupt, but I have a radiotelephone message for Miss Pickerell. From earth."

Miss Pickerell tore open the long, official envelope Mr. Rugby handed her. The yellow sheet of paper inside looked like an ordinary telegraph form. It said:

MISS LAVINIA PICKERELL

C/O COMMANDER M. M. MANBOROUGH SPACE FORCE LUNAR BASE MOONPORT THE MOON NO CHANGE IN COW'S CONDITION OUR HOPES ARE PINNED ON YOU YOUR NIECES AND NEPHEWS SEND THEIR BEST HUMWHISTEL

Miss Pickerell silently read and reread the message.

"I've been here three times," Mr. Rugby went on. "You were sleeping, Miss Pickerell, I didn't want to disturb you. And I knew there was nothing special in the message. They let me read the copy at the Communications Center."

Miss Pickerell showed the yellow piece of paper to Commander Manborough. He read it and gave it back to her. Miss Pickerell put it into her knitting bag. She polished her glasses with a neat white handkerchief that she took out of the bag and patted a loose hairpin into place.

"Well," she said finally, "at least I know that my cow is no worse."

"We'll be needing to contact you again within the next few hours. Where will we find you, Miss Pickerell," asked Commander Manborough.

"Beg pardon, again, sir," Mr. Rugby said. "May I suggest that Miss Pickerell might like some refreshments? My assistant in the cafeteria has just made a fresh pot of tea."

"Excellent idea!" Commander Manborough replied. "We'll be in touch with you there, Miss Pickerell."

He turned to walk toward the ramp.

Mr. Rugby came to attention and saluted stiffly. Commander Manborough returned the salute and dashed off.

"Should we take my short cut?" Mr.

146

Rugby asked. "Or do you prefer the cross-tunnel car, Miss Pickerell?"

"Your short cut," Miss Pickerell said. Privately, she didn't think the short cut was one bit faster than the cross-tunnel way. But she wanted to be polite, and Mr. Rugby was trying so hard to be helpful.

He chattered all the way to the cafeteria. Miss Pickerell was too tired to pay much attention to what he was saying.

The tea tasted better than it had the last time, and Miss Pickerell decided to have another cup. Mr. Rugby also gave her what he called an Eclipse Special, which was a slice of sponge cake covered by a ball of ice cream. Miss Pickerell said that she liked the idea of using words from astronomy on the moon menu.

After he finished clearing the food away, Mr. Rugby joined Miss Pickerell at her table. "My assistant's on the job now," he told her. "I'm free until tomorrow."

"Where's the telephone?" Miss Pickerell asked, her mind on the call she was expecting.

"In the back," Mr. Rugby replied. "But I've turned up the bell amplifier. We'll hear it good and loud when it rings."

Miss Pickerell sighed, thinking of the hours that must pass before she could even hope to hear about Pumpkins. She looked in her knitting bag for the scarf she was trying to finish, then remembered that she'd left it in her room.

The cafeteria was nearly empty now. The young assistant behind the counter stood looking at the clock. He had red hair and reminded Miss Pickerell of Dwight, her oldest nephew.

Miss Pickerell looked at the clock, too. It seemed to her that it had stopped. She knew this was nonsense. It was just that the time was passing so slowly.

"Are you sure we can hear the telephone where we are?" she asked Mr. Rugby.

Mr. Rugby's mouth closed suddenly. Miss Pickerell realized that she had interrupted him right in the middle of a sentence. She had not even known he was talking. She felt terrible.

"It's all right," Mr. Rugby said. "I know how hard it must be for you. I'm a restless man myself and I hate waiting. Would you like to play some checkers, Miss Pickerell? My assistant and I often play when it's slow like this in the cafeteria."

Miss Pickerell agreed. Mr. Rugby got the checkerboard and put it on the table. Miss Pickerell set up the checkers.

The telephone rang twice while she and Mr. Rugby were playing. Each time, Miss Pickerell jumped up, her heart pounding. But the calls were not for her.

Mr. Rugby was a very slow player. Miss Pickerell nearly lost patience with him when she had to wait as long as ten minutes between some of his moves. And she beat him every time.

"Another round! Another round!" he insisted, at the close of each game.

By the end of the fifth game, Miss Pickerell decided she simply could not go on. She looked up from the board to tell Mr. Rugby that this time her decision was final.

At precisely that moment, the door to the cafeteria opened. Commander Manborough and Dr. Guffey walked in. Miss Pickerell's heart felt as though it were turning somersaults. She trembled violently when she tried to stand up.

But Commander Manborough and Dr. Guffey knew how terrible this suspense must be for her. Dr. Guffey smiled broadly as a signal that the news was good. And Commander Manborough called "Fine! Fine!" to her right across the cafeteria.

"Pumpkins is not all well yet, you understand, Miss Pickerell," Dr. Guffey explained, when he came closer and could talk to her. "The signs are definite enough, though. He's responding. It's the antibiotic he needed. The mold growth was a light bluish-green, something like Penicillium in color, but an altogether different shape."

Commander Manborough kept pumping her hand up and down. "You've made history, Miss Pickerell!" he said.

"What about my cow?" Miss Pickerell

asked. "What do I tell Dr. Haggerty? He said that if it was the right antibiotic, more could be made in test tubes and—"

"Right!" Dr. Guffey beamed. "Once we know the arrangement of atoms in an antibiotic, we can put them together and produce the same antibiotic—in any quantity we want."

"That's all taken care of, Miss Pickerell," Commander Manborough said. "Dr. Guffey has already analyzed the contents of this mold. He had also radiotelephoned the formula to Mr. Humwhistel for transmission to Dr. Haggerty."

"Then Dr. Haggerty may be delivering the formula to an earth laboratory this very minute!" Miss Pickerell exclaimed.

"Exactly!" Commander Manborough replied. "And now, Miss Pickerell, if you'd like to remain as our guest on the moon for the next three months, we can send you back by passenger ship. Otherwise, you will have to start making preparations for your return. The cargo ship leaves today. We hope you will decide to stay."

"I'd rather go," Miss Pickerell said. "I want to see my cow. Thank you just the same, Commander."

"I thought you'd say that," Commander Manborough said. "When can you be ready, Miss Pickerell?"

"As soon as I get Pumpkins and my satchel," Miss Pickerell said.

Commander Manborough insisted on carrying both her satchel and her knitting bag, and Mr. Rugby followed with her spacesuit. Dr. Guffey went ahead to get Pumpkins ready.

The officer on duty in the supply room helped Miss Pickerell and Commander Manborough step into their spacesuits. Dr. Guffey, holding Pumpkins, and Foster, his arms full of packages, were waiting outside at the moonmobile.

"They're presents," Foster explained. "For the folks at home." He put all the packages except one in the back of the moonmobile.

"This one," he said, giving her the small box he still held in his hand, "is from all of us, for you. It's a prize rock in our mineralogical collection. It comes from the exact center of the Copernicus crater."

"Foster, I don't know how to thank you," she said, staring at the rock which sparkled with all the colors of the rainbow.

Miss Pickerell could just imagine how proud the governor would be when it was exhibited at the state fair next year.

"It's we who have to thank you," Commander Manborough said. "And now, let's get going."

Dr. Guffey began to shake hands with Miss Pickerell and then said, if Commander Manborough didn't mind, he'd come along to see her off, too. He, Miss Pickerell, and Pumpkins sat in the rear, under the bubbletop. Pumpkins ate vitamin snaps all the way back to the spaceship.

A lunar patrol officer stood ready to check Miss Pickerell in. He smiled and gave her a package of moon labels. "You can paste them on your luggage," he said. "To show everybody where you've been."

Miss Pickerell asked if there was time for her to take some pictures.

"You've got plenty of pictures of me," Foster said. "Every seven seconds when you pushed that flash, you took my picture at the same time."

"You've got me, too," Commander Manborough said. "My ship and me inside."

Miss Pickerell decided to take one picture of Dr. Guffey and one of the lunar patrol officer.

Co-pilot Thurston Williston came over to tell Commander Manborough that they were about ready to leave.

Miss Pickerell was just saying good-by when another moonmobile rolled into view. Major Finch got out and ran forward to shake hands with Miss Pickerell. He was followed by the stout, spacesuited figure of Mr. Rugby, who carried a bright crimson rose in a plexiglas box.

"Our first moonflower," he said. "I talked the head gardener into giving it to me for you."

Mr. Williston gestured to Miss Pickerell from the spaceship that it was time to go aboard. She thanked Mr. Rugby quickly and, holding Pumpkins close, climbed up the ladder.

The hatch slid shut behind her. One of the crew members strapped her and Pumpkins onto the contour couch. The launching rockets fired and the ship rose. Miss Pickerell waved to the people who were becoming smaller and smaller, until she could no longer distinguish them.

"Good-by, moon," she said.

Then she leaned down to look happily at Pumpkins' bright eyes and moist, pink nose. "We're going home," she whispered, "home to our earth!"

16

A Rousing Welcome

Two days and eleven and one-half hours later, the cargo spaceship *Cow* drifted down onto the Square Toe County landing field. Miss Pickerell unstrapped herself and Pumpkins and began to get up off her con- tour couch. She had to make several tries before she could manage it. The pull of gravity kept forcing her down. She also had to get used to the full weight of her body when she followed Mr. Williston through the ship's airlock and out onto the ladder.

The cheering began the instant she set foot on earth. Afterward, Rosemary told her that everybody kept quiet while she was climbing down the ladder because they were afraid of frightening her. Miss Pickerell said. "Pooh! I've gotten quite used to going up and down ladders."

All of Miss Pickerell's friends and relations were at the landing field to greet her. Deputy Administrator Horace T. Blakely, carrying a bulging briefcase, was the first to congratulate her. He was accompanied by a television reporter who popped a microphone in front of her while everybody shouted, "Speech! Speech!"

Miss Pickerell was too overwhelmed for the moment to say anything.

The governor, wearing gloves and a shining black top hat, smiled at her proudly. "Miss Pickerell," he said, "you've put this state on the map. The new antibiotic has already halted the epidemic."

Everybody applauded and began to sing the state song.

"I couldn't have done it without the help of Lieutenant Foster Esticott, our own Mr. Esticott's fine young cousin. And of course not without Pumpkins," Miss Pickerell added.

Mr. Humwhistel helped Miss Pickerell take Pumpkins out of his spacesuit. Miss Pickerell handed Mr. Humwhistel her knitting bag to hold while she raised Pumpkins up high so that everybody could see him. Pumpkins meowed lustily.

The crowd cheered.

Miss Pickerell tried to take off her gloves and push back her space helmet. The governor's wife came over to help her. Everybody applauded again.

Mr. Humwhistel, waving a piece of paper in his hand, edged through the crowd. He shook Miss Pickerell's hand and whispered something to Deputy Administrator Blakely.

Mr. Blakely called for silence. "I have an important announcement to make," he said.

The television reporter moved up to him. Mr. Blakely leaned down to speak into the microphone.

"Ladies and gentlemen of the television audience," he said, "we have just received a message from the moon. In recognition of Miss Pickerell's contribution to moon science, it has been decided to name a crater in her honor. From now on, the crater adjoining the place where the moon spores were found will be known as the Lavinia Pickerell crater."

The crowd went wild with applause.

The governor smiled and asked Miss Pickerell whether she had brought back any new additions for her famous rock collection. Mr. Williston held up her precious Copernicus rock and moonflower. They were greeted with admiring "Ohs." Cameras whirred and clicked. The *Square Toe Gazette* took the most pictures.

"Your attention, please!" the governor shouted, as a television reporter stepped up to him. Everybody stopped talking. The governor stroked his mustache.

"Miss Pickerell is the star of this show," he said grandly. "And I'm going to get her to speak to you in just a few minutes. But before that, I'd like to do three things. First, let me call on Miss Pickerell's 'space detective,' the man who furnished the clues for her mission to the moon, my very good friend, Mr. Humwhistel."

Mr. Humwhistel hurried forward. He fumbled in his pocket for a sheet of paper, which he unfolded, pushed his glasses back on his nose, and read: "For her distinguished service in space exploration, Miss Pickerell has been elected a full member of the Society of Lunar Pioneers and awarded a Certificate of Honor by the Association of Space Scientists.''

A roar of applause followed this speech.

"Now," the governor said. "it is my privilege to present some young people who never stop talking about our famous Miss Pickerell.''

Miss Pickerell's nieces and nephews, all seven of them, marched up front. Euphus spoke into the microphone. He announced that Miss Pickerell had been chosen by all the Boy Scout and Girl Scout troops of Square Toe County to be the permanent chairman of their "Be Kind to Animals Week.''

A rousing cheer filled the air.

"And now," the governor said, pausing dramatically for an instant. "If you will all move to the right—''

He could not continue. As the people moved, Miss Pickerell saw the little red trailer in the rear. Dr. Haggerty was driving it toward her. Her cow, the silver bell tinkling gently around her neck, stood under the little canvas awning. Miss Pickerell rushed to the trailer and threw her arms around the neck of the cow, who mooed contentedly.

The governor led Miss Pickerell back to the microphone. She was not able to talk at first. She had to get rid of the lump in her throat. Then she spoke about how happy she was to have helped her cow. And she told how touched she was by all the honors that had been bestowed on her.

"I never dreamed of anything like this in my life," she said. "A crater named after me!"

Best of all, she was pleased by her election in the Boy and Girl Scout troops, she said. It showed how much the children cared about animals. "And loving animals is one of the nicest things that can happen to any child," she declared.

Miss Pickerell concluded her speech by stating that as adventurous as it was to be on the moon, it was even more thrilling to be home again on the green earth of Square Toe County.

ABOUT THE AUTHORS
AND ILLUSTRATOR

ELLEN MACGREGOR was born in Baltimore, Maryland. She created Miss Pickerell in the early 1950s and wrote four stories about her, as well as boxes full of notes for future adventures. She died in 1954, and not until 1964, after a long search, did Miss P. finally find Dora Pantell.

DORA PANTELL has been writing "something" for as long as she can remember—magazine stories, scripts for radio and television, and books for all ages. Ms. Pantell does her writing in lots of places, including airplanes and dentists' waiting rooms. She says that she most enjoys writing the Miss Pickerell adventures. There are now twelve titles in the series, all available in Archway Paperback editions.

Among Ms. Pantell's pastimes are reading non-violent detective stories and listening to classical music. She lives in New York City with her three cats, Haiku Darling, Eliza Doolittle and Cluny Brown.

CHARLES GEER is an author as well as an artist, and has illustrated more books than he can count. He enjoys hiking, camping and sailing, and lives near Flemington, New Jersey with his wife, four children and a cat.